JULIA

ANGEL CREEK CHRISTMAS BRIDES

LILY GRAISON

Julia
Angel Creek Christmas Brides book 2

Copyright © 2018 by Lily Graison
All Rights Reserved

ISBN - 9781729421307

Cover Design by
https://www.wickedsmartdesigns.com

Visit Lily's website at www.lilygraison.com

JULIA

PROLOGUE

Hiding behind a happy smile when your heart is grieving never gets easier. Julia stared out the window, watching the falling snow as memories of all those loved ones no longer with them brought tears to her eyes.

The laughter of the children gathered in the room was the only thing that kept the sadness from consuming her. It was Christmas Eve after all, and there was no room for frowns today.

Charity, one of her oldest and dearest friends, was telling her account of how they all came to be in Angel Creek and slowly, the memories of that first Christmas chased away her blues.

She heard her name and looked over her shoulder. Charity was staring at her. So was every child present. Her grandchildren and those of her friends were sitting in a semi-circle in the middle of the room, all with expectant looks on their faces.

Rebecca, her oldest great-granddaughter sat up on her knees. "Come tell us about when you first met grandpa."

"Yes!" Hannah yelled, a happy smile on her chubby face. "Tell us about you and grandpa Bailey."

They'd heard the story dozens of times but never seemed to grow tired of hearing it, which suited her fine. She never grew tired of telling it. Remembering the past gave her a chance to reminisce about those who had already left them.

She crossed the room and took a seat, then laid a finger to her chin as if thinking. "Well … let me see. I believe it was right after the war." She grinned at Charity. "Someone had the absurd idea of us becoming mail-order brides so Charity, Ruby, Sarah, and Anna dragged me kicking and screaming all the way out here."

Anna laughed. "Liar."

Julia settled back in her seat and closed her eyes, the memories filling her mind's eye. "Angel Creek Montana was nothing like Charleston…"

CHAPTER ONE

November, 1865

The town was tucked into the shadow of several mountains and the crooked streets were filled with mud. The squat buildings lining the road through town were nothing more than square boxes of unadorned wood planks, several of them leaning a bit to one side—unless the weeks of travel while staring out the window to take in the scenery had permanently damaged her neck to the point everything looked tilted.

Julia Hamel stepped out of the stagecoach and pulled the hood of her cloak tighter around her neck as a gust of blistering wind whistled through the valley. She blinked against the falling snow and took in the small town that was to be her home and was unimpressed.

She certainly wasn't in Charleston anymore.

A deep inhaled breath to clear the musty smell of multiple bodies crammed into a too-small stagecoach filled her lungs with the scent of woodsmoke, and surprisingly, clean, fresh air. It

3

wasn't the salt-tinged sea breezes she was used to but it was pleasant all the same.

She saw very few people on the wooden walkways in front of the buildings but those she did see were staring at them as if they were some sort of spectacle. She supposed they were. Their brightly colored dresses stood out amongst the garments of the people on the sidewalks. Most of the ladies she saw were in simple gingham dresses, unadorned boots, and close-fitting bonnets that covered so much of their head she could barely see their faces.

The town was eerily quiet. The sound of gulls flying over the harbor was missing, as were the sounds of horses and carriages traveling over cobblestone streets. All she heard here was the occasional voice, wind as it whistled through the valley and every so often, the ting of a blacksmith's hammer. It seemed like a ghost town compared to Charleston. That gnawing feeling in her gut telling her she'd made a mistake in following her friends in this crazy adventure ached anew. Perhaps she should have never left South Carolina. Her father told her she was being foolish and she hated to admit, he may have been right.

"This way ladies. Someone will see to your bags and make sure they get to where they need to be."

Julia turned as she saw the others start walking away and only half-heard what the man escorting them from the stagecoach station said. She followed quietly, tiptoeing through the snow to prevent her kid boots from getting wet and was glad when their small party stepped onto the wooden sidewalk that ran in front of the buildings lining the street.

Her stomach grew more queasy with each step and by the time she stopped in front of a small church, she was praying her meager lunch stayed down.

She was the last to ascend the steps leading into the building and found it was quite warm inside and pleasantly quaint. Several men stood by a fireplace built into one of the sidewalls and those nervous butterflies returned the moment they all turned to look at them. Somewhere in that group of men was her new husband, a stranger she was to give herself to freely. She suddenly felt ill.

The next several minutes consisted of introductions and Julia had the sensation of being outside herself. As if she was watching from some great distance. It was fatigue. She knew it was when she couldn't even remember walking to the front of the church and joining hands with a complete stranger about to marry him.

She heard her friends talking quietly to their soon to be husbands and sneaked a peek up at her groom. The instant she did, her heart started to race.

Don't be fooled by his good looks, Julia. He could be deranged and end up killing you. Or you could die out here in the middle of nowhere by freezing to death. Or be eaten by some wild animal. You could be taken by Indians or trampled by wild horses!

Julia closed her eyes and inhaled deeply in an attempt to calm her nerves. The scent of burning wood from the fireplace filled her head, along with the faint smell of gun oil and fresh cut cedar, the last two clinging to the man in front of her.

The small sounds the others were making and the soft ping of sleet as it hit the church did nothing to distract her from the "what-ifs" whispering through her head on repeat. She opened her eyes and stared at her hands held in the firm grip of a man she knew nothing about other than his name.

The preacher, Reverend Tilly, was fumbling his way through their marriage ceremony and she listened with half an ear. She knew her duties as a wife. She was to love, cherish and obey her husband and she'd try her best to do just that—eventually. Once she knew who this stranger in front of her was.

"Miss Julia?"

She blinked and focused her attention on the reverend. "Yes?"

"Do you take this man as your husband?"

"Oh!" She took a peek over her shoulder to find her friends

looking at her. Her face heated as she said, "Yes, I do." Julia peeked up at her soon to be husband, Matthew Bailey, he'd introduced himself as, and felt the butterflies in her stomach take flight as she briefly met his gaze. He certainly wasn't what she'd been expecting.

A mail-order bride could end up with any sort of man and the man her mind conjured had been old, possibly poor as dirt, and skinny to boot. Her friends had reassured her that wouldn't be the case and she was glad to see they had been right. Seeing this man step forward and say her name had nearly caused her knees to buckle. Matthew Bailey didn't fit the picture she'd painted in her mind of her future husband at all. He wasn't old, nor was he skinny, and to her great surprise, was quite possibly the best-looking man she'd ever seen.

Which made those nervous butterflies all the worse. He was too good to be true. Her luck was never this good. Something was bound to go wrong.

She peeked a glance up at him again. He was staring at her, his blue eyes taking in every inch of her face. Of all the men who showed up to marry them, Matthew was the most handsome—at least she thought so. Not that the others were unpleasant to look at, Matthew Bailey just seemed—more. More rugged. Stronger built. More—manly.

Maybe it was the breadth of his shoulders or the close-cut beard or the work-worn calluses she could feel on the palm of his hands. Or maybe she was so used to men in fancy dress suits with tailored vests that seeing a man in simple trousers and a long-sleeved shirt made him appear to be more—brawny.

And yet—she was going to marry the brute. What if he was mean? He outweighed her by at least a hundred pounds. He could—

"I do."

His voice drew her from her thoughts. She inhaled a deep

breath, let it out and took another. *Breathe, Julia. Everything will be all right.*

"You may kiss your bride."

Julia raised her eyes, meeting Matthew's gaze and when he just stood there staring at her, she wondered if he was having the same doubts she was.

Long seconds ticked by before he leaned toward her, that kiss the preacher said he could give her moments away, and Julia didn't realize she was holding her breath until he kissed her on the cheek.

Her heart started pounding as she took a breath. He gave her hands a small squeeze and said, "I don't wish to rush you but there's a storm blowing in and we have a long ride back to the house. You need to say goodbye to your friends so we can be on our way."

The parting was bittersweet. Her girlfriends all seemed to be happy. If they were as nervous as she was, they hid it well. There were more than a few tears shed but she was cheered up by the knowledge that Anna would at least be close by. She lived outside of town, as Matthew said he did. The others would all be within walking distance of each other. She envied them for that. They wouldn't feel as isolated as she already did. They'd have each other for support and she'd have—she turned her head to where her new husband stood by the door. He was watching her.

She gave Anna a tight hug, then embraced Sarah, Charity, and Ruby each in turn and told them she'd see them as soon as she was able.

Then she faced her husband and crossed the room to where he stood.

"Ready?"

"Yes." She tried to smile but failed miserably as he helped her into her cloak. When she'd secured it, he opened the door, a blast of cold air hitting her so fast she shivered. Once again, she was reminded she wasn't in South Carolina anymore and knew by the time winter was over, she'd be homesick for the milder temperatures she was used to.

The light dusting of snow that had been on the ground when they arrived had deepened. Matthew took her hand and helped her down the slick steps and to the waiting wagon. The carpet bag she'd used to store her things in while traveling was sitting in the back and several blankets were stacked on the seat.

In all her twenty-two years of life, she'd never ridden in an open wagon. She'd seen her share of the inside of carriages and surreys but this plain wooden wagon was so—ordinary.

Life as she'd known it was about to change drastically.

Matthew helped her onto the seat and Julia sat nervously as he walked around to the other side and climbed up to sit beside her. He lifted one of the blankets and opened it, offering it to her before taking the reins in hand—and then they were moving.

Julia covered her legs with the blanket then looked back at the church. The others were coming outside and her heart clenched painfully in her chest seeing them. They'd been together for so long now. Leaving them felt so—final.

"You'll see them again, I promise. I'll not keep you from them."

Her bright green eyes locked with his for a brief moment. With effort, Matt tore his gaze from her and stared at the snow-covered road.

The screaming matches he'd had with his sister over the past week replayed inside his head as the gentle clomp of the horse's hooves churned up dirty snow and ice. Those fights seemed a bit childish now.

He'd balked at the idea of a mail-order bride the moment Prudence told him about it and once he found out she'd sent away for one without his knowledge, he'd yelled, cussed, and threatened to choke the life out of her. But the moment he got his first look at those women, he'd had to rethink his plans of torturing Prudence for the rest of her life.

The women who stepped inside that church looked nothing like what he expected them to. If the expression on the other men's faces were any indication, those ladies weren't what they had envisioned them to be either.

Any woman desperate enough to pick a husband from a paper did so because she had no other prospects and likely never would, but the five ladies that traveled all the way from South Carolina to marry left them all speechless. They weren't bedraggled or homely. They were—well, too fancy for Angel Creek and he'd studied them all, bewildered, wondering which one was to be his new wife—and forgot all about telling her there had been a mistake, that he couldn't marry her after all. No, he'd said his new bride's name and when the tall one with dark hair took a step forward and locked eyes with him, he'd forgotten how to breathe. He might still be mad at Prudence for deceiving him but he couldn't be mad at how the entire ordeal ended. What man would when his new wife was simply—breathtaking.

Matthew glanced over at her. She looked half frozen. He picked up another blanket, opened it and draped it around her shoulders, something in his chest pulling tight when she gave him a small smile and said, "Thank you."

She pulled the blanket in tight around her slim frame. Julia was tall for a woman, not that he minded. He'd kissed his share of girls when he was younger and being over six-foot-tall meant every single time he did, he'd had to bend nearly double. When he'd placed a soft kiss to Julia's cheek in the church, he'd only had to lower his head. It was a nice change, so was her voice. She was soft-spoken, the cadence making her seem as delicate as she appeared. She was lovely and as much as he hated to admit it, for once, Prudence had been right. He was indeed pleased with his new bride.

❄

The extra blanket Matthew placed around her shoulders warmed her in only a few minutes. Other than her thanking him, neither had said a word and the silence was deafening. It gave Julia time to reflect on her journey from Charleston, though, and she was still questioning her decision to come out west. Even more so now as the wind felt like it was cutting her to the bone and the snow that was falling didn't look to be letting up. If anything, it was falling harder, the path they were taking slowly disappearing under several inches of fresh powder.

This certainly wasn't what she'd been expecting. When Charity arrived at their weekly sewing circle with a copy of the Groom's Gazette in hand, she'd thought her friend had been teasing them about wanting to be a mail-order bride—until she saw the determination in her eyes. She'd been quite serious and it didn't take long for the others to sit up straight and listen to her idea intently. By the time Charity told them of her plan, they'd all been excited, rambling on about what an adventure it would be, and when everyone turned to her, for one brief moment, she'd thought they'd all lost their minds.

Then reality sank in.

They weren't getting any younger and the prospects in Charleston were next to nothing now that much of the city was in ruins and most of the eligible young men hadn't come home after the war ended. There was nothing left for her there, for any of them, really. Unless she wanted to grow old and become a spinster, she had no choice.

They'd all been happy when she agreed to join them—under the condition they all went to the same place. She got her wish, but as the wagon traveled over the bumpy road further away from town, she realized she should have been more specific. They were all in the same town but she wasn't going to live anywhere near them. What would become of their weekly sewing circle now?

She pulled the blanket Matthew placed over her shoulders tighter around her and peeked at him out of the corner of her eye. Would he take her into town every week? For some reason, she doubted it, so didn't ask. She supposed there was time for such conversations later.

The trip across the prairie seemed to take forever. They passed very few houses and every minute that ticked by took her further away from the others. The road up ahead forked in two different directions. Matthew steered the wagon toward the right. The worn tracks from numerous wagons traveling the same path weren't as heavy here.

Trees lined the road on both sides and she had to admit, with ice and snow coating the limbs, it was breathtaking to behold. She could hear the rush of water too and looked for the source of it, barely seeing it through the trees and the snow that continued to fall.

"That's Angel Creek. It runs directly behind the house."

Julia didn't reply, her focus still on those brief glances of water she could see. Long minutes later, they came to a wide wooden bridge that crossed the creek, the horse and wagon clanking across it, and as much noise as they made, it wasn't enough to drown out the sound of the water as it rushed over the rocks.

Large sections along the creek banks, and nearly every rock she saw, had frozen over, small waterfalls being carved into the ice, and it was the most beautiful thing she'd seen on the entire trip from the east coast. Had it not been so cold, she would have been content to sit there half the day watching it.

Once they reached the other side of the bridge, the ranch came into view. She wasn't really sure what she expected but— this wasn't it.

They'd read the listings in the Groom's Gazette of men in

Angel Creek looking for a wife and once she found out her new husband was a rancher, she'd tried to imagine what his home would look like. She'd had the impression of land filled with animals and wide-open barren fields, the grass trampled down to nothing as hordes of animal hooves marred the ground. The wide-open fields were here, but the animals weren't. For as far as she could see, it was nothing but rolling hills all the way to the mountains in the distance.

The house was two stories with a porch that ran along the entire front of it. Not quite the wide veranda around her father's home, but close. She could picture herself there on hot summer days while she and her friends gossiped over tea, assuming they would all come out this far if she invited them.

A large barn and several outbuildings were off to the left. A few men were walking around and more than a few stopped to look their way as Matthew set the foot brake on the wagon and jumped to the ground.

He came around to her side before lifting a hand to help her down. When her feet hit the snow-strewn grass, the fatigue she'd been trying to ignore since stepping off the stagecoach caused her knees to buckle. She gasped and stared wide-eyed at Matthew when he caught her before she hit the ground.

"Are you all right?"

"Yes," she said, heat filling her face. "I guess the trip has taken more out of me than I thought it had."

"Understandable." He helped her upright again, holding on to her until she was steady. "Can you walk?"

Could she? She was still shaky but she wasn't so weak she couldn't walk.

She apparently waited too long to answer. Matthew scooped her off the ground and into his arms before she could get a single word out and she stifled a startled yelp as he started for the house.

It took every ounce of willpower she had to relax and not

protest him carrying her, especially when he asked her to open the front door, then proceeded to carry her inside and up a flight of stairs to a bedroom at the end of the hall.

The room wasn't as large as the one she'd had back home but it wasn't small by any means. Matthew set her on the bed and stepped away and Julia's heart was once again pounding. The scent of peppermint hung in the air and she instantly longed to see her father. His room had always smelled of sweet treats too and she wondered if her new husband had a stash of candy hidden somewhere. Her father hid his in the top drawer of his dresser and she'd snuck in many times as a child to take a piece.

She glanced around the space, taking in the furnishings. This was definitely a man's room. There was nothing feminine about it at all. It was all brown wood and dark colored curtains, the bedspread she sat on was a dark color as well. She'd remedy that soon enough, though. It was nothing new curtains and the marriage quilt she spent months making wouldn't improve upon. It just needed a woman's touch.

She spotted the trunks she'd shipped ahead of her departure from Charleston stacked against the wall. "I see my things arrived."

Matthew nodded his head and moved to the door. "They were delivered last week. I'll bring your traveling bag in once I've seen to the horse. Rest for a while. Take a nap or just relax." He started to close the door but stopped. "Unless you're hungry. I can rustle up something for you to eat if you'd like."

"No, thank you. I think I'd rather rest for a while."

He nodded his head once, then left the room, pulling the door closed behind him. As she listened to his footsteps growing more distant, her pounding pulse slowed to normal.

The bed underneath her caused the butterflies she'd finally won control over to take flight again. She was twenty-two years old and had never been kissed. Had never even been in a room alone with a man, and now she was sitting on a bed she was to share with one. To be intimate and lie with, naked.

Her heart was fluttering like a caged bird in seconds at the thought. Sarah had told her what to expect on her wedding night and she had let more than a few thoughts pop into her head, right or wrong. Now, she was a new bride and ready or not, come nightfall, Matthew Bailey would come to her bed, and despite Sarah's reassurance that everything would be fine, she was absolutely terrified.

CHAPTER TWO

Matthew could hear the squeaky wheels of a wagon coming down the road as he stepped out onto the porch. He knew it was Prudence without even looking.

Since the day he found out Pru had sent off for a mail-order bride in his name, he'd been plotting ways to make her life as miserable as his was. Killing her would brand him a murderer and he'd been willing to live with the consequences but knew that wasn't possible now. Not once people saw his new wife. They'd think he was an idiot for even complaining about what his sister had done and probably hire the ornery busybody to find them wives, too.

Her wagon rounded the bend and came into view a few moments later and she threw her hand up and waved when she saw him. He walked down the steps and into the yard toward his wagon and hoped she had no intentions of staying or introducing herself to his new wife, but something told him that's the very reason she risked coming out in the storm. If she didn't live so close by he would have been angry she even tried. The storm moving in was probably the only reason she hadn't been at the church.

Prudence meddled in his affairs too much. She gossiped as if it were her job and liked to make decisions without his knowledge and as infuriated as he'd been when he found out what she'd done, he'd begrudgingly have to admit—for once—her sending off for a mail-order bride without his knowledge hadn't turned out so bad. Not that he'd ever tell her he thought so. As far as his sister was concerned, he was still mad as hell.

She was grinning when she pulled her wagon up beside his own and set the foot brake. "I ran into Pete on the way over here. Talk in town is those southern belles were a sight to behold! The fanciest things to hit Angel Creek since Elijah Oliver built his eatery and laid those lace tablecloths down."

"I'm still mad at you, Pru."

She laughed. "Liar." Jumping to the ground, she rounded the wagon and looked toward the house. "She in there?"

"Where else would she be?"

"Back in town looking for a husband. I do recall you saying you weren't marrying a woman you've never set eyes on."

He pulled the blankets from the wagon seat, folded them and tucked them under his arm before reaching in to grab Julia's bag. "Well I couldn't leave her stranded in town after she traveled halfway across the country to get here, now could I. Besides, if anyone else in town would have wanted a wife, they would have sent for one, not hung around the church in hopes an extra would just happen to be there."

She was smirking at him. She didn't believe the sorry excuse he'd been trying to convince himself of any more than he did. He scowled at her. "She's resting, so go home. You can talk to her later."

Prudence pulled her cloak up around her neck when a blast of cold air swept over the valley. "Is she pretty?"

He ignored her question as he turned to the house and set the blankets and the carpetbag down, then headed back to the horse and wagon.

"She is, isn't she?" She laughed. "And all that fuss you made about me sending off for you a wife—"

"—Has caused me more trouble than I needed."

"Hogwash." She waved a hand in the air as if his words meant nothing. "I saved you from the biggest mistake of your life, is what I've done."

Matthew took the horse's reins, walking the animal to the barn. Prudence dogged his every step, talking nonstop and he ignored her, glancing back at the house as he pulled the barn doors open and all he could think about was Julia, who was more than likely asleep in his bed.

"Are you even listening to me?"

He motioned for one of the ranch hands to come take care of the horse then turned to his sister. "Not really, why? Did you say anything different from the same old conversation we've been having since you started this whole mess?"

"You're an ornery old goat, anyone ever tell you that?"

"You, at least once a week."

She crossed her arms over her chest and narrowed her eyes. "When can I meet her?"

"A week from Tuesday."

She scowled. "I'm serious—Matthew."

"So am I—Prudence."

She clenched her jaw once, her lips pursing. "Fine. I know how it is when a man takes a wife so I'll give you some privacy but," she pointed a finger at him, "don't think to keep me away forever. She may be your wife but she's my new sister and I've waited a long time to have another woman in this family and you won't deny me that or so help me, Matt, I'll skin you alive!"

She turned on her heel and stomped off toward her wagon, climbing up and giving him a rude gesture with her hand before flicking the horse's reins and heading back down the road. He watched her until she was out of sight then turned back toward the house. He should take Julia's bag up to her. See if she needed anything.

Something in his chest clenched tight. Prudence had made a real mess of things. He hadn't told a soul he had a wife coming, secretly hoping she'd never show up, but Julia's arrival made his life a bit more complicated. Pru may have thought she was doing him a favor by sending away for Julia but she made things worse. Now, not only did he have a new wife to learn to live with, he had to figure out how to tell the girl he promised to marry that he already had a wife.

A noise jarred Julia from sleep. She opened her eyes, and for a brief moment, didn't know where she was.

The day's events came back to her in a rush and she sat up, taking in what she assumed was her new bedroom, if her trunks in the corner and her carpet bag that now sat on top of them were any indications.

You're a married woman, Julia. The words whispered through her head as she turned to sit on the edge of the bed.

She still felt weary. The long trip across the country had been tiresome and she would have loved nothing more than to crawl into bed and sleep for a solid week. She stood and crossed the room to her trunks instead and spent the next twenty minutes sorting through her things, spreading the marriage quilt she'd spent so much time making across the bed, and tried to find a suitable dress to put on. The traveling suit she was wearing was hot and confining and her corset was digging into her ribs. If she could just loosen it a few inches she knew she'd feel better.

A quick glance around the room showed there was no dressing screen and she had no desire to strip down to her corset without one, regardless of the fact she was now married.

A ladder-back chair sat next to the dresser. She pulled it to the door and braced the back of it under the door handle. It wasn't much but it made her feel better.

The water pitcher in the corner was full, the water so cold it took her breath as she bathed her sweaty skin. When she was clean and in a fresh dress, she smoothed a hand over the wrinkled material and looked out the window. It was still snowing, the ground nearly covered completely now.

She could see clean to the mountains in the distance from this side of the house. Several men were walking out by the barn and a small building a few hundred yards away seemed to be the hub of activity with men coming and going. She wasn't sure what the building was and wondered if that was where the ranch hands lived. She'd have to ask her new husband.

Turning away, she crossed the room and removed the chair from under the door handle and went to explore the house.

Matthew Bailey's home wasn't as grandly appointed as her father's had been but it seemed sturdy and well lived in. It lacked a woman's touch but that could be easily remedied over time. There was a total of two bedrooms upstairs, a formal sitting room downstairs, a small room that appeared to be some sort of office tucked underneath the stairs, a dining room, and a small room holding nothing more than a cot and a large trunk off from the kitchen.

Julia inspected the house, noting things that needed attending as she went. When she reached the kitchen, nervous butterflies took flight as she looked at the stove. A pot sat on top of it, and if the scent filling the room was any indication, something was cooking. Was she not expected to do that?

She glanced at the clock. It was later than she'd expected it to be. Maybe her new husband got tired of waiting for her to get up and started supper without her. With her cooking skills, it was probably a good idea he had.

Bess, the family cook back home, had taught her all she could in the short time she'd had before Julia stepped on that train to travel west. She knew she'd eventually be required to cook and even though she was eager to try, she couldn't help but be grateful the duty had not been placed on her today.

The door close to the cabinet swung open. Julia stared at Matthew as he came inside. He stilled the moment he saw her, then shut the door, removed his hat and coat and hung them both on a peg nailed into the wall.

"Did you sleep well?"

Julia nodded. "Yes, thank you."

He crossed to the cabinet and washed his hands, then grabbed a hand towel sitting on the counter. When he turned to face her, they both stood there in the silence, the only sound that of the ticking from a clock in the other room and the steam releasing from whatever was cooking on the stove.

Matthew was the first to move. He crossed to the stove and lifted the lid from the pot and gave the contents a stir. "I wasn't sure what you liked. I can't guarantee this is the best you've ever eaten but I've not keeled over yet from eating my own cooking."

Julia smiled, the tension in her shoulders easing at his flippant remark. "I'm sure it will be fine. I'm hungry enough to eat an old shoe."

"Well, luckily for you, I was fresh out of those." He picked the pot up and set it on the table. "Have a seat. I'll grab some bowls."

Julia glanced back at the dining room once before sitting at the small table in front of a large window. It gave her a perfect view of the snow and ice encrusted creek just beyond the yard and she imagined it would be beautiful with spring flowers dotting the bank. As much as she enjoyed seeing the snow, she was eager to spend long, lazy summer days with her feet in that creek while mountain breezes blew through the valley.

She watched Matthew grab bowls and cups and eating utensils, noting where everything was. A small part of her felt bad he'd had to cook. She was sure that was a task he'd taken a wife for and if so, she'd failed on her first day as a new bride.

He returned and filled her bowl, then sat across from her. She looked down and smiled. Chicken and dumplings. One of the first things Bess taught her how to make. Thank goodness he liked them.

Her glass was filled with cool water before Matthew finally looked over at her.

"It smells good."

He picked up his spoon. "Not as good as my gramps used to make but it's passable."

They spoke little while they ate and if Julia had to guess, she'd say he was feeling as nervous and clueless as to what to talk about as she was. Regardless of the fact they were man and wife, they knew nothing about each other besides their names.

Halfway through the meal she dabbed at her mouth and glanced his way. "Do you live here alone?"

He nodded. "Yes. Well, other than a few ranch hands that live out in the bunkhouse." He refilled his water glass, then her own. "I've a sister who lives close by. Her name is Prudence and she's as nosey as the day is long." He grinned. "She came 'round not long after we got home in hopes of meeting you. I suspect she'll be back sooner rather than later."

"I look forward to it."

"You may think differently once you meet her." He chuckled. "She means well but comes off very abrasive. Our mother died when we were young so Pru took over the household duties and ordered us about as if she wasn't still a child. My gramps found it amusing so he told my pa to just let her do as she pleased. I think gramps just wanted her to take over the cooking for him, which she eventually did."

"And where do gramps and your father live now?"

He stilled and stared down at his bowl. "They're gone. Gramps died ten years ago and my father was killed, along with Pru's husband, four winters ago."

"Oh, I'm sorry."

21

He nodded but said nothing else and neither did she. The circumstances around his father and Prudence's husband's death must be painful. Something in the expression on his face said it wasn't something he liked to think about.

They finished eating and cleared away the dishes, then Matthew showed her around the house, even though she'd peeked into all the rooms herself when she came downstairs. They ended up in a small parlor off from the front door. There were a few seats scattered about the room. Matthew added a few more logs to the burning embers in the fireplace before saying he'd bring more wood in. When he'd left her alone inside the house, she studied the room. It was much like the bedroom—all dark wood and dark furnishings. Luckily, she'd brought enough things with her to brighten the place up and as soon as the sun rose tomorrow morning, she'd do just that.

The chores inside the barn were nearly finished when Matt stepped in out of the cold. Silas and Orin looked his way as he shut the barn door, both of them wearing identical grins.

"Go ahead and say what you want, then be done with it."

Silas laughed. "I thought you went to town to tell whoever it was that showed up to marry you that there had been a mistake."

"I did."

"And?"

"And—" Matt removed his hat, scratched his head and put the hat back on. "And it didn't work that way."

"Is she as pretty as she looked from a distance?"

Pretty was too mild a word to describe her. "She's very pretty."

"You got lucky," Orin said. "My cousin over in Bixby got a mail-order bride and she was missing most of her teeth and had one eye that wandered a bit." He closed the gate on the horse stall he'd been in and swung the rope over the rail so it'd stay shut. "She's a good cook though, so according to my cousin, that makes up for her poor looks."

Silas grinned. "Were the others as pretty as your wife is?"

Matt nodded. "Yes. They were all handsome women. All friends, from what Pru said when she told me about sending away for a bride. I think we all got lucky."

"More so come nightfall."

Silas and Orin both laughed, teased him until he felt heat scorch his face, and finally had mercy on him and wished him a good night before leaving.

In the silence of the barn, their teasing hit him hard. He might be married to Julia but until they consummated the marriage, it was just words on a piece of paper. Was she expecting him to come to her bed tonight? Or did she expect him to give her privacy until they knew each other better? It wasn't as if he could ask. He'd not embarrass her or himself by being so bold but— what was he supposed to do?

He sighed and scrubbed a hand over his face. The desire to scream at Pru again for this mess burned hot in his gut, especially when he thought of the position she'd left him in. Things with Julia were awkward enough but what was he supposed to tell Cora?

They'd been friends for years and often talked about never marrying but something had always rung untrue about her words. He knew she'd been lying about not wanting a husband when she told him she'd accept a wedding proposal from him. Her words were said in a teasing manner and he'd done the only thing he could to not embarrass her—he said he would. He'd foolishly told her that if she hadn't married by her twenty-fifth birthday, that he'd marry her and every time he saw her, she reminded him her birthday was coming very soon. He'd had less than six months to make good on that promise—a promise Pru had nearly come unhinged about every time she saw Cora. He knew without a doubt Pru ordered a bride just so he'd not have to marry her and that plan had put him in an awkward position.

If he'd told Julia he couldn't marry her because of Cora, she would have been stranded here with nothing but the clothes stored in her trunks. Had Julia not been a beauty, he would have still felt duty-bound to marry her only because Pru had promised he would.

Not marrying Cora did nothing other than hurt her feelings. She still had a home to live in. She still had her family to take care of her and despite what he'd told Pru, there were men in town that would take a wife if one were available. Cora had just never given anyone the chance to court her—no one but him, that is.

He sat down on one of the hay bales, took off his hat, and ran his fingers through his hair. Seemed as if life was always kicking him in the teeth and today was no exception. One catastrophe after another had plagued him for years, and with Christmas just a few weeks away, the nightmares were returning.

The memories of that day came back in a flash and he closed his eyes to force them away. He scrubbed a hand over his face when the screams echoed in his head again and he paced across the barn, trying to push the memories back where they belonged but the sound of Prudence screaming wasn't something so easily forgotten. He still heard it in his dreams, saw the horror on her face as her new husband disappeared and he knew, just like him, she hated this time of year as much as he did.

Maybe that's why she sent for Julia. So she'd have someone to distract her from the fact her life had been destroyed and she'd yet to put it back together completely. Well, that and she disliked Cora more than anyone else on earth and would never accept her as part of their family. She might have wanted a new sister but, as always, Prudence made sure it was someone she chose. He just wished she would have told him about it before Julia had been sent money to travel west. Or before Cora had teased him about making wedding plans because he had no doubt she was planning a wedding and he had no idea how to tell her he already had a wife.

A wife he was now supposed to go inside and bed.

He groaned and braced his hands on the top of the horse stall. Maybe he should sleep out here. Surely freezing to death would be less painful than fumbling through his wedding night. He'd not bedded a woman in more years than he wanted to think about. Julia was undoubtedly untouched—or he assumed she was —so crawling into her bed would be embarrassing for the both of them so … did he just do it and get it over with or wait until he was sure she was ready?

Julia brushed through her hair one last time and stared into the small mirror she'd sat on the dresser top. Her reflection in the glass showed her face paler than it should have been and she knew it was nothing more than nerves making her appear so pallid.

She pushed her hair behind one ear. Should she braid it or leave it down? "Leave it down," she whispered. "It might distract him from the fact you're practically naked." A glance down at her gown caused her heart to skip a beat. Would it make her appear too wanton to wear such a garment? The material was so thin she knew it would take very little for him to realize she had nothing on underneath it. The flowers she'd embroidered around the neck were small and not enough to hold anyone's attention for long, especially not a man who was ready to bed his wife.

Groaning she laid a hand to her stomach when it seemed to do a small flip. She was working herself into a good tizzy standing there. She turned to the bed. Should she wait for him there, underneath the blankets? Or just—stand here so he could see all of her once he came into the room? No. Having to look him in the eye, knowing he could see her through the gown, would be too embarrassing.

She hurried to the bed and pulled the blankets back, crawled in and laid down. She fixed the gown, pulling it down her legs then thought better of it. Should she pull it to her waist? She cringed, closed her eyes and sighed. "I don't know what I'm doing."

Julia strained to hear anything other than the wind rattling the windowpanes. Not a sound could be heard, which meant either her new husband was a very light walker or he hadn't come inside yet. It was full dark, well past time to turn in for the night. Maybe he was waiting for her to get settled, then he'd come in.

Leaning over, she extinguished the lamp and laid back down, listing to the wind whistle past the house. Regardless of whether she was ready or not, come morning, she'd be Matthew Bailey's wife in every sense of the word.

CHAPTER THREE

She woke up alone. The blankets beside her were untouched, still tucked in as they had been the night before and something in Julia's chest clenched tight.

Matthew hadn't come to her and she was still as virginal as she had been when she'd crawled into bed the night before. She wasn't sure how to feel about that. Should she be happy she'd been spared the embarrassment she was sure to have come with the act or disappointed her new husband hadn't wanted her? A better question would be, if he didn't want her, then why did he marry her? Why did he send away for a bride to begin with?

The answers never came so she eventually rose and dressed, braided her hair and pinned it up, then looked out the window. The sun was barely cresting the mountains but it was light enough outside to see it was still snowing. Nothing stirred, but the windows in the small building she'd seen the day before, and assumed was the bunkhouse Matthew had told her about, were lit.

She ventured downstairs, peeking into the empty rooms as she went. She wasn't sure where Matthew had slept. She didn't see him and a part of her was glad for it. She wasn't sure what she'd say to him once she did. Facing him would be awkward now, more so than if he'd come to bed the night before.

The kitchen stove was cold when she entered the room. She spent long minutes filling it with wood, then lighting it, waiting for it to start burning hot before inspecting the larder. There was a basket of eggs on one of the shelves, along with milk, the cream still sitting on top. There was salted ham and so many bags of flour she'd be able to bake enough biscuits to feed the entire town of Angel Creek.

Jars of canned vegetables and fruit preserves filled the space. Seeing them, she realized her job as wife would be much harder than she thought. She didn't know the first thing about preserving food for the winter. The most gardening she'd done was planting a flower or two. She had no idea how to grow food in quantities enough to feed someone all winter long.

She blew out a breath and made a mental note to ask about it later and pulled everything she needed from the shelves. There was an old flour sack on a nail hammered into the wall by the larder door. Grabbing it, she wrapped it around her waist then started on her first meal as a new wife. By the time everything was cooking, she was covered in flour, sweating like a mule, and secretly hoping Matthew didn't come out from wherever it was he'd slept to catch her in such disarray.

She peeked out the window toward the barn. There was still no movement on the other side of the frosted panes. The snow wasn't falling as hard now but a thick blanket of it covered every surface she saw.

Julia grabbed plates and cups and was turning to the table when she saw someone exit the barn. She panicked the moment she saw them coming toward the house. She dropped the plates and cups and tried to dust the flour from her clothes, then pushed the stray curls dangling by her face out of her eyes and wiped the sweat from her brow.

Peeking back out the window, she saw the man turn and head in the opposite direction and she sighed in relief. She had no idea if it was Matthew or not but she wasn't ready for him to come inside. She'd planned this first meal in her head so many times now and she wanted everything to be perfect. Her looking so unkempt from cooking one simple meal wasn't how she wanted him to see her.

Picking the plates and cups back up, she set the small table by the window and was laying utensils out beside each plate when she got the first whiff of burnt bread. She gasped and ran to the stove.

Opening the door, she choked on the black smoke boiling out and grabbed a towel to pull the pan of biscuits out—then cringed. "No, not today!"

They were ruined.

Her shoulders sagged as she stared at them, tears burning the back of her eyes. *You're going to make a horrible wife, Julia. You should have never agreed to this and just stayed in Charleston.*

She sat down heavily in one of the kitchen chairs, staring at the biscuits for long moments before dusting off her apron, misery making her chest hurt. "Your new husband wasn't interested in bedding you and once he finds out you can barely cook, he'll be hauling you back to the stagecoach station." She groaned and covered her face with both hands. "You should have never come."

"They look just right to me."

Julia screamed and jumped out of the chair at the voice, turning to see an old man standing by the cabinet. He was nearly as tall as she was with hair of pure white and a beard and mustache to match. He grinned and said, "Didn't mean to startle you," before inhaling deeply, then laying a finger to his nose. "My smeller isn't what it used to be. Tell me, is there onion in those fried potatoes?"

Julia stared at him for long moments as her racing heart

slowly returned to a normal pace and finally nodded her head. "Yes."

"Thought so." The old man grinned and walked to the stove, leaning over it to look into the other pots. "Them's some good looking vittles ya got cooking. Matt's not eaten so fine a meal since he told Pru to stop coming by to mother him. "

Julia wasn't so sure about that. She glanced around the room. The old man was alone as far as she could tell. How he'd come inside without her hearing him was a mystery, though. She finally lowered her hand and took a calming breath.

He eyed her, squinting a bit. "You going to be all right?"

"Yes." Julia smiled to try to ease her discomfort. "I didn't hear you come in so you gave me quite a fright."

"I suppose I would have. Apologies."

Julia waved away the last of the smoke and stared at the biscuits. The old man did as well. "Just cut away the worst of the black bits and they'll be fine. Matt likes them well done."

"These are a bit more than well done."

"Nothing wrong with a crispy biscuit. Matt prefers them that way."

Julia wasn't sure she believed that, especially when she saw the look in the old man's eyes. There was a bit of mirth dancing in his blue irises and she wasn't sure if he was laughing at her or her disbelief that her new husband would prefer a burnt biscuit. Whatever the reason, and despite the fright he'd given her, Julia felt oddly at ease with this stranger.

She scraped the bottoms and cut the burnt places off the biscuits as he said and placed them on a plate, brushing off the black crumbs best she could, then stared at them, unhappily. They looked awful. "Are you sure he likes them like this?"

"Positive."

She exhaled a breath and nodded her head. "I'll take your word for it, then. Thank you." She turned back to the stove, gave the milk gravy a stir and slid it back from the heat, then glanced over to where the old man was standing. He was gone.

"What in the world…" Julia looked around the kitchen, then at the door. "Hello?" She walked into the main room and heard a door open and close behind her. Walking back into the kitchen, she found her new husband washing up by the sink.

"Morning."

"Good morning." Julia brushed a hand over the front of her dress.

Matthew dried his hands and looked to the stove. "Smells good."

Julia willed her racing pulse to slow and walked back to the stove. "I wasn't sure what you liked."

"I'll eat most anything."

Julia glanced at the biscuits. *I'm counting on it.*

She grabbed the folded bits of cloth she'd found to handle the hot pots and reached for the pan-fried potatoes as she heard the legs of one of the chairs scrape across the floor. She set the pot on the table and Matthew said nothing as she laid the rest of the food out, never moving until she'd taken her seat.

"All my favorites," he said before grabbing a spoon and started dishing food onto his plate.

The tension in her shoulders eased as he started eating, more so when he grabbed two of the nearly burnt biscuits, tore them into small pieces and covered them with the milk gravy she'd made. He didn't hesitate in picking them up so, apparently, the old man had been right. Her new husband didn't mind burnt biscuits.

Maybe Bess had been too critical when she said she was a terrible cook. It didn't seem as if Matthew shared her opinion and come end of the day, as long as her new husband liked her cooking, that's all that mattered.

She was a horrible cook. Matthew swallowed the food in his mouth and washed it down with the most bitter coffee he'd ever tasted and tried not to grimace.

He could see Julia out of the corner of his eye. She was watching him, so he picked up another of the nearly burnt biscuits and drowned it in lumpy gravy and took another bite. It was edible, at least, but just barely.

She finally lowered her head and started eating. There was flour in her hair and a dark smudge of something on her cheek—burnt bread remnants if he had to guess—and despite all that, she was still the prettiest thing he'd seen in ages. He'd get used to her horrible cooking given time. He just hoped he survived until he did.

They ate in silence for several minutes, the only sounds to be heard were that of the wind and the scrape of forks on the plates. He choked down another gulp of coffee and looked over at her. "Did you sleep well?"

"Yes. Thank you."

He sure hadn't. The spare room off the kitchen had the most uncomfortable bed in the whole house but he hadn't wanted to wake her by climbing the stairs and sleeping in the spare room. Truth be known, he knew if he'd climbed those steps, he'd be tempted to open her door and invite himself inside and he didn't need to be told how bad an idea that would be. He and Julia may be married but they knew nothing about each other and he was sure, him inviting himself to her bed, wouldn't be the best way to start a marriage.

The silence continued and he'd nearly cleared his plate when the back door opened. He turned to see Prudence grinning at him and he rolled his eyes. "How did you get over here?

"Old man Nichols let me borrow his sleigh. I don't care what people say about him, the man is a saint in my book."

"Pete just—let you take it, by yourself?"

She scowled and shut the door. "I'm not incapable of guiding a few horses through the snow."

"No, but I've never known him to let anyone else use that sleigh."

She shrugged a shoulder and removed her coat and hat, hanging them on one of the pegs nailed into the wall. "Well, he let me. And if he were thirty years younger, I'd be tempted to marry him."

Prudence grabbed a plate and cup from the shelf and set them on the table before pulling out a chair and sitting down. She filled her plate with the remaining scrambled eggs and fried potatoes, then grabbed one of the biscuits. She gave it a hard look before cutting the bottom off and laying it in her plate. She picked up the pot of gravy, spooning it onto her plate as she said, "That old stove can be tricky. The left side heats up hotter than the right for some reason so shove your pan all the way over or you'll end up with burnt bread every time."

Julia's cheeks turned a pretty shade of pink. She glanced at him quickly before saying, "I'll keep that in mind."

Prudence set the pot down and hooked a thumb his way. "Since that one's suddenly lost his ability to speak, I'm his sister, Prudence."

"I've not lost the ability," Matt said, "Just the desire."

She snorted a laugh. "That's a first." Prudence took a bite, her eyes widening a bit before chasing it with the coffee—then choked. "Damnation, that's bad." She coughed, then stood and carried the coffee pot to the back door and poured it out. "They not teach you southern belles how to fix coffee in the South?"

Julia's cheeks reddened again as she flicked a quick glance his way. "We drank tea more than coffee."

"And let me guess," Pru said, "You never had to fix it yourself."

When Julia lowered her head to stare at her plate, Matthew threw a glare in Pru's direction. "If the only reason you're here is to insult my wife, then go home."

The ornery woman had the nerve to grin at him. "I wasn't trying to insult *your wife*, little brother, just stating a fact. My apologies, Julia. I'm bossy and blunt so don't take offense to anything I say."

Prudence filled the pot with water and grabbed the coffee grounds, measuring out what she needed and telling Julia which spoon to use, then set it back on the stove to heat. When she took her seat again, she picked up her fork and said, "So, how are you liking Montana so far?"

Julia folded her hands into her lap. "It's colder than I expected but the snow is pretty to look at. I've only ever seen it once before but that was only when it was falling. It never laid on the ground."

"Well, get used to it. There's snow in Montana more often than not. You'll eventually get to where you hate it as much as I do."

Matthew listened to them talk, and as loathe as he was to admit it, he was grateful Pru showed up when she did. The awkward silence before she waltzed into the room was making him uncomfortable and he knew without being told Julia felt the same way. The look on her face and her barely eating told him as much.

He blew out a breath and cleaned his plate, thoughts of his new wife a constant echo in his mind as he listened to her and Pru talk. Better her than him. He wasn't good at talking to women. Never had been. Not even to Cora. He never knew what to say to them. He knew nothing about the things that interested a woman and pretending he did only made the situation more uncomfortable. He knew about ranching and cattle and not much else. Hell, he didn't even know how to court a woman properly. He was sure there was more to it than showing up with a hand full of pretty flowers. Talking would be expected at some point and that would bring him right back to where he was now. Struggling for something to say to a woman who seemed just as tongue-tied as he did.

"You listening to me, Matt?"

Prudence thumped a knuckle on the table and he snapped out of his musing. He met her gaze and as always, a bit of mischief danced in her eyes. "Not really."

She huffed out a breath. "I said Julia needs proper boots and warmer clothes. We could take her into town since I have Pete's sleigh."

Take Julia into town? Matt ran his gaze over her. The dress she wore was a bit fancy for working around the house and he didn't think she had on sturdy work boots with a frock like that on. Her boots were probably those silk things he'd seen Cora wearing, the ones with buttons all the way up the side. They weren't made for tromping around in the snow, that's for sure. She'd need something suitable for the ever-changing Montana weather.

He nodded and stood when the coffee pot lid started to rattle, crossing to the stove to refill his cup. "All right, but you'll have to go without me. I have missing cattle and we have to see where they've wandered off to." He turned back to the table. "Just put everything on my tab and tell the Weston's I'll be in on Friday to settle the bill."

Pru grinned and he knew she was about to hit him where it hurt—his bank account.

Matthew had insisted they take the blankets he'd offered her the day before in the wagon and she was glad he'd made them do so, otherwise her face would be frozen with a permanent smile. The biting chill in the air caused her skin to ache and made her eyes water but the sleigh ride across the Montana prairie was the most exhilarating thing she'd done in—well, forever, really.

The horse kicked up snow with every step he took and

LILY GRAISON

managed to keep up a fast enough pace for the ride to be thrilling. After the morning she'd had, a delightful romp across the prairie was exactly what she needed.

She didn't have to be told the breakfast she'd made had been barely edible. Matthew had cleaned his plate but she was sure he'd done so as to not be rude. The gravy had almost congealed and the biscuits … she cringed. The old man had lied about Matthew liking his biscuits near burnt and she planned on giving him a piece of her mind next time she saw him. Not that she really had reason to be mad at him. She shouldn't have been so gullible. Who in their right mind wanted to eat burnt biscuits?

"You're awfully quiet."

Julia glanced at Prudence and smiled. "I've been accused by many of being too quiet, especially around people I don't know. My friends were the social butterflies. I was more of a wallflower."

Prudence laughed loud and boisterous. "You don't look like a wallflower. I always pictured someone fitting that description as dowdy and unattractive and you are neither of those things."

Julia smoothed out the material of her cloak. There was a compliment in there but wasn't sure if it was sincere or not so she didn't acknowledge it. She'd been called many things but attractive wasn't one of them. She was too tall, or too quiet and to most—too plain. Had she been anything else, she would have married years ago. She changed the subject, pulling the hood of her cloak in closer to her face. "So, tell me about Matthew. What sort of things does he like?"

Prudence gave her a sly look and grinned. "He likes you. I knew the moment he ran me off yesterday."

"He ran you off?"

"Yep. I came by to meet you right after you got out to the ranch and he wasn't having it. Said you were resting and wasn't to be disturbed."

36

"Oh, well, that is true. I did rest once we arrived at the ranch. That doesn't mean he likes me, much."

Pru laughed. "Yes, it does. If he didn't like you, he wouldn't have cared if I disturbed your rest. He would have let me barge up those stairs and wake you without a thought to your wellbeing. But he didn't. He wouldn't even let me near the house which means, he likes you. Plus, I've seen the way he looks at you. Or I should say, the way he doesn't look at you. He's trying too hard not to stare which tells me, he likes what he sees."

She wasn't lying. Julia had noticed him glancing away as quick as she looked at him but thought it meant he wasn't interested. Him not coming to bed the night before had been another sign. He seemed to be putting distance between them—well, until she remembered how he'd picked her up and carried her into the house the day before. Or how he'd done the same not an hour before when he lifted her from the porch and carried her to the sleigh. He'd claimed he didn't want her boots to get ruined in the snow but was it more than that? Did her husband like her more than she thought he did?

The hazy outline of buildings in town came into view and Prudence urged the horse faster. "I'll introduce you to any townsfolk we run into and show you where your friends are living. We can visit with them if you like, as long as it doesn't start snowing again.

"That would be nice, thank you."

"There's good folk living in Angel Creek. Well, everyone but Cora. That one you'd be better off not knowing."

The words were said pleasantly enough but something in Prudence's eyes said otherwise, as did the expression on her face. So, who was Cora? And why would meeting her be so bad?

CHAPTER FOUR

The mercantile was rustic compared to the merchant shops in Charleston but with Prudence's help, Julia was able to find a good, sturdy pair of boots made for trekking in the snow and a few, simple dresses. Warm gloves and a hat were paired with a wool cloak that came with a fur hand muff and according to Jeremiah Weston, the owner of the mercantile, she was ready to take on the wilds in the Montana Territory as well as anyone else did.

She'd questioned the new purchases when they were being wrapped. She knew nothing of Matthew's finances. His home wasn't as grand as her father's had been but it was by no means a poor man's shack but spending so much on her so soon seemed—wrong. She would have been happy with the new boots but Prudence had insisted, especially when she picked up the cloak. It was the only one like it in the store. It was fur lined and heavy, and the price tag on it had made her mouth fly open in shock. She'd refused but Prudence had only laughed off her concern.

When her newly purchased items were wrapped, Prudence took her to the Apothecary in town and a small shop that sold baked breads and sweets and they stayed long enough to eat their fill of pastries before washing it down with coffee. Julia wasn't sure she'd ever grow to like the taste of it but the shop owner, Ona Jenkins, had sweetened it with a bit of cream and sugar and she was able to get it down much better.

Back on the street, Prudence had pointed out all the other businesses in town, most of which they didn't stop at. In the center of town, she showed her where her friends lived. The desire to run to their door was strong but she didn't want to intrude so soon after arriving. Besides, light snow flurries were beginning to fall again and she didn't want to get stuck in town.

They headed back to where they left the sleigh and she was introduced to everyone they saw on the way. When they were at the end of the street, Prudence grabbed her arm. "I see the sheriff. Wait here a minute. I need to ask him something."

Julia waited a whole three minutes before turning toward the sleigh and hurrying down the sidewalk. The wind felt as if it were cutting through her bones and she'd never been so cold in her life. Her new cloak was wrapped in paper and why she hadn't put it on was beyond her. It was stupid, really. She should have donned all her newly purchased things for no other reason than they were warmer than anything she owned.

Her feet were near frozen by the time she made it to the end of the row of buildings lining the road. The sleigh was still where they'd left it and Julia tossed her packages inside and had grabbed the side to climb in when a light in the corner of her eye caught her attention.

The last building on the street had a pretty, ornate sign hanging above the door that read, Thompson's. The light she'd seen was an open door on a stove in the center of the store, a young boy standing in front of it tossing in more wood.

Julia looked down the street for Prudence but didn't see her. She blew into her hands, stared at the cold sleigh, then turned back to the shop. Surely Prudence would look for her here if she came back and didn't see her.

A bell above the door made a small tinkling of sound when

she walked inside. The interior of the building was so warm, Julia felt it immediately and made a beeline for the potbelly stove sitting in the middle of the room, thrusting her hands out to warm them. It would certainly take time to get used to the cold.

A glance around the shop told her she was inside a Millinery and dress shop. She smiled. This reminded her of Charleston. The shop was filled with color, dresses by the dozens displayed along the walls, ribbons, and lace in every color imaginable hung from pegs and small displays and the hats were as fine as the ones she'd seen back home. For such a small town, she was surprised to see such finery.

There was a bit of shuffling toward the back of the building. Julia turned her head as a woman slipped through a doorway covered by a curtain. She stopped when she saw her and said, "Hello. I didn't hear you come in."

"That's quite all right. I must admit I initially came in only for the warmth." She glanced around the store. "But now that I see these beautiful dresses, I'll be sure to come back."

The woman smiled. "You're new to Angel Creek. I don't think I've ever heard that accent before."

"Yes, I only arrived yesterday. I'm originally from Charleston."

"Well, it's very nice to meet you." The woman crossed the room to where she stood. "I'm Cora Thompson."

Cora? Was this the "Cora" Prudence had mentioned? "It's nice to meet you as well, Cora. I'm Julia Bailey."

"Bailey?" Something in her eyes brightened as she said the name. "Any relation to Matthew Bailey?"

"Yes. He's my husband."

Cora was a pretty woman whose stature was on the short side. Her hair was blonde, her eyes blue, and she seemed the sort of person Julia would indeed invite to tea. But as Cora stood there looking at her, something in her eyes changed, her smile quickly vanished and her lips pressed together forming a harsh line across her face.

The door opened before she could ask if anything was wrong and they both turned. Prudence's eyes were a bit wide as she stood there staring at her. "Julia," she said, "I've been looking for you." She flicked a glance at Cora and nodded her head in greeting. "Cora."

Julia had dealt with socialites in Charleston long enough to pick up on subtle clues and it didn't take but a few seconds to realize there was something volatile between these two. Cora's smile had completely vanished, she was stiff-backed, her chin raised, and the look in her eyes told her she didn't want Prudence in her store.

Prudence didn't look much different except for the tiny smirk on her face. "I see you've met my new sister-in-law, Cora. I'm sure you two will be fast friends."

Cora scowled. "Somehow I doubt that."

Something was wrong. He could see it in both their faces as they climbed out of the sleigh. Julia didn't spare him a glance as she trudged through the snow toward the house and Prudence blew out a breath when she looked up and saw him.

"What happened?"

Pru shook her head. "Now, what makes you think something happened?"

"The look on your face, not to mention Julia's."

Prudence reached in for the packages Julia couldn't carry. "I saw the sheriff in town and ran to tell him about your missing cattle and to ask if anyone else had mentioned any missing livestock and when I got back, Julia was waiting for me inside Thompson's.

His heart seized for a brief moment. "I'm almost afraid to ask."

Pru handed him the rest of the packages. "Nothing happened. Not really, but you don't have to worry about telling Cora you can't marry her, now. Julia did that for you." She laughed. "You should have seen Cora's face. I wish I had been inside when she said she was your wife. I would have paid money to see it."

Matt bit back a curse. "Did Cora say anything?"

"No, but she didn't have to. The look on her face was enough for Julia to ask me a dozen questions on the way home, though—all of which I refused to answer—so you have that inquisition to look forward to baby brother."

Prudence climbed back into the sleigh and took hold of the reins. "I'd love to stay but I need to get this thing back to Pete."

"Liar."

She chuckled and said, "Good luck," before flicking the reins and pulling away from the house.

Julia wasn't in the kitchen when he walked in and it only took a few seconds to hear her upstairs. He debated laying the packages down and running back to the barn but he'd never been a coward, so he headed for the stairs.

Her bedroom door was open when he reached it and he peeked inside before clearing his throat. "May I come inside?"

Julia nodded. "It's your house."

"Our house now," he corrected as he stepped into the room. He set the packages on the end of the bed and looked at the things she'd already unwrapped. Thick socks and new boots lay amongst the brown paper they'd been wrapped in along with a thick pair of gloves and one of Mrs. Tilly's knitted scarves. He touched the large package he'd carried in. "I hope this is a warmer cloak."

"It is." She reached for it, pulling the paper away before lifting the cloak for him to see. "I thought it was a bit too extravagant but Prudence insisted. We can return it if it's too much."

The cloak was one he'd seen before. It was longer than most and was lined with thick, white fur. Cora had made mention of it on several occasions, wondering why the Weston's insisted on purchasing clothing when her parents' shop was just down the street. The Thompson's hated the competition, especially when that competition had things much nicer than anything they made or sold in their store. Knowing Pru, she made Julia get that cloak just to snub Cora.

"It was a smart choice," he said. "You're not used to the cold. That extra warmth will do a lot to keep you warm."

They stood in silence for long moments as Julia folded the brown paper her things had been wrapped in and rolled the twine that held them closed. When she'd finished, he cleared his throat. "Would you like me to show you around the ranch? Or you can rest if you'd prefer."

She picked up a pair of the socks. "I think I'd like to look around. I'm not even sure where the well is."

"All right. I'll wait for you downstairs." He hurried back to the kitchen and stood by the counter to stare out the window. His thoughts went to Cora and he wondered what she thought about Julia's announcement. Even though she now knew, he'd have to pay her a visit and explain and he dreaded the thought of it.

Julia was quick about changing her boots and was wrapping the cloak around her shoulders as she entered the kitchen. When she pulled the hood up and had it tied, she said, "I'm ready when you are."

He ushered her outside and helped her down the steps, then stopped and pointed to the right. "Just beyond that tree is the well, but don't worry about fetching any water while there's snow on the ground. Silas refills the stove reservoir in the bunkhouse every morning and fills a bucket for the house as well so, more than likely, it'll be sitting on the counter when you get downstairs."

He motioned her forward a bit and pointed out past a row of trees. That big area in front of the fence is where the garden sits in the summer and there's a grove of apple trees on the other side of the house close to the creek."

"Is all this land yours?"

Matthew nodded. "Yes. There are a couple hundred acres out past the fence line."

Julia stared in the direction of the creek. The hood on the fur-lined cloak framed her face and a few wisps of her dark hair had come undone, the small curls brushing her cheeks drawing his attention. A simple look was all it took to remind him again of how lovely she was. The conversation with Cora would be unpleasant but coming home to Julia would make it less painful.

"You're a cattle rancher, right?"

Her voice drew him from his thoughts. "Yes. I have a couple hundred head at last count."

"And where are your cattle?"

He rubbed a hand over his beard and pointed toward the south pasture. "They're out that way. There's a hill just behind the barn so you can't ever see them unless they come closer to the house."

"Oh, I see. I've never been around cattle before. Are they dangerous?"

He chuckled. "Not unless they're running and you're in the way."

She smiled and he noticed a small dimple in her cheek. How had he not seen that before? It drew his attention to her lips and the moment he looked at them, he wondered what they'd taste like. He'd stood at the bottom of the stairs the night before, staring into the darkness instead of climbing the steps like he'd wanted to and regretted his decision now. He'd thought her lovely the moment he saw her but now, with snow falling around her fur-lined face, she was mesmerizing.

She caught him staring and he looked away, taking her arm and leading her to the barn, showing her where the chicken coop was on the way.

Silas and Orin both looked up when he pushed the barn doors shut behind them, both men tipping their hats toward Julia.

"Ma'am." Silas turned and started their way. "I'm Silas. You ever need anything, you just give me a yell."

"And what he can't do for you, I can." Orin crossed the barn, his usual grin in place. "Names Orin."

"It's a pleasure to meet you both, gentlemen."

Orin grinned bigger. "That's some accent you got there."

"Oh? I didn't realize I had one."

Both men laughed before saying their goodbyes and headed back into the stall they'd been in. Julia turned in a small circle, taking in the rest of the barn, and stopped when she got to the stall with the colt. "That's the newest addition around here," Matt said. "He was born a few months ago."

Julia crossed to the stall and peered inside, the smile on her face big enough he could see that dimple again. "He's beautiful." She reached out, then jerked her hand back. "Is it all right to touch him?"

"Yes, he's not skittish." He clicked his tongue and reached out until the colt crossed the distance between them.

Julia's smile was infectious. He watched her pet the colt, her eyes bright and with every passing minute, his ire at Pru for sending away for Julia lessened. He was still upset she went behind his back but looking at Julia, he couldn't be completely sorry she had, even though his new wife was too fragile for the wilds of Montana. He knew nothing about her background but if he had to guess, he'd say she'd not had much reason to ever get dirty. She was too-refined. Her hands were free of calluses, her complexion as clear and smooth as porcelain. She'd not ever had to work in the sun and if he had to guess, he'd say she'd been waited on, her every desire met by someone else's hand.

"Does he have a name?"

Her voice drew him from his musings and he focused on her face. "No. I never got around to giving him one."

She frowned. "He has to have a name." She rubbed the colt

45

behind the ears, laughing when he moved closer and snuffled at her face.

Matt leaned against the railing and propped his arm along the top board. "If you'd like, you can give him one."

Her eyes widened? "Really?"

He nodded. "Absolutely."

The smile on her face widened. "Then he's Sir Lancelot." She peeked over at him, her cheeks turning pink. "It's a silly name, but as a child, I always wanted a horse of my own. I asked for one every year on my birthday but we lived in the city and father didn't want the trouble of having to stable him somewhere."

Matt reached out to stroke the horses head when the colt moved his way. "Well, then consider him a wedding gift." He stepped back from the gate and pulled the rope from around the post and opened it, then grabbed the horse brush from the table by the wall. "Your horse hasn't been tended to today so," he handed her the brush, "here you go."

Her smile had waned somewhat but her glassy eyes were enough to tell him why. She blinked a few times and stepped into the stall, laid the brush to the colt and started to brush him. She looked back over at him a few minutes later. "I have no gift to give you."

Matt's gaze roamed her face and landed on her lips. "You agreeing to come all the way out here to be my wife is gift enough."

Don't cry. Do. Not. Cry.

Julia repeated the words like a mantra as she laid the brush to the colt's snowy white coat and started brushing him. Matthew was watching her, his arms propped on the top rail of the stall, and it took every ounce of willpower she had not to weep like a baby.

It was silly, her reaction, but the gift had been given so freely, so selflessly, that Julia had learned something very valuable about her new husband. He was not a brute, nor was he cruel. Instead, he was kind and giving, his handing over the ownership of the little colt proof of that.

"Where is his mother?"

"She died right after he was born."

A sharp stab of pain pierced her heart at the news. "Oh, how terrible." She brushed his mane while rubbing her free hand down his neck. "Poor thing." The colt turned his head, snuffling at her hand.

"He gets more attention than any other animal here because of it so, he may be alone in the world, but he's a very spoiled animal."

She was glad to hear it.

Silas stopped by the railing and spoke to Matthew in soft tones. Julia watched them, using her husband's distraction to study him. Her assessment yesterday of him being nice looking didn't fully describe him. Matthew Bailey was, quite honestly, the most handsome man she'd ever seen and the way he looked at her—

A shiver crawled up her spine and she looked away when he turned his attention back to her.

"I've something that needs my attention. Will you be all right alone for a few minutes?"

"Oh, certainly. Go do what you must."

The other ranch hand, Orin, joined Silas and Matthew and she watched her new husband until he shut the doors behind him, blocking the cold blasts of air from pouring into the barn. In the silence she petted the colt, grinning as the name *Sir Lancelot* whispered through her mind again. Her father had accused her of fanciful notions on more than one occasion, her penchant for reading too many books, the main culprit he'd said, but she'd never paid him much mind. There was nothing wrong with

47

wishing for a knight in shining armor, complete with white steed and the little colt being white made it all the more amusing.

Her new husband didn't exactly fit the classic description of the heroes in those books she'd read but he did get one thing right. He'd given her something she desired and expected nothing in return.

"He's going to be a looker when he's full grown."

Julia squealed and startled the horse as she spun around on her heel. Her heart felt ready to burst from her chest as she saw the old man again and scowled at him when he began to laugh. "That's the second time you've sneaked up on me."

He walked a full circle around the horse, inspecting him from every angle. "I was a horse man back in my day. Bred them by the dozens. This old barn has seen more horse births than anything else. Matt found more money in cattle, though. Can't fault him for it. He's done a fine job around here." He gave her a sly grin. "Got himself a pretty little bride too."

"Thank you, but please make some noise next time. You're going to give me heart failure."

He laughed again and readjusted his hat. It wasn't the type Matthew and the ranch hands wore. The old man's hat was much different—older in style, but she supposed it would be. He was quite ancient himself.

Julia took a few calming breaths and started brushing down the horse again. "I should be very upset with you."

"Why's that?"

She gave him a pointed look. "You know very well, why. Those burnt biscuits were barely edible and Matthew forced himself to eat them."

He laughed so loud, she was surprised none of the animals reacted. "I wish I could have seen the look on his face."

"Well, I wish I didn't remember it. He'll probably never eat my cooking again."

The old man continued to laugh at her expense and as mad as

she should be at him, she oddly wasn't. She stepped around the horse to his other side and continued to brush him. "I don't remember your name."

"I don't remember you asking for it."

"Oh, well, I suppose I didn't. I'm Julia."

"Abraham, but you can call me Abe."

"Very well. It's nice to meet you, Abe."

He looked around the barn when the wind gusted and whistled through the boards. "Sounds like another snow shower is fixin' to blow in."

"I hope so. I enjoyed watching it fall. We never saw snow much in the south."

"I suppose you didn't. It's tricky out here. It can blow up into a blizzard in a blink and melt just as fast."

"Do you think it will hang around until Christmas?"

Abe raised his hand and scratched the side of his nose with his thumb. "I imagine it will."

Julia grinned. "I've always dreamed of a white Christmas."

"You enjoy the holiday, then?"

"It's one of my favorites."

"Mine as well. My Ester loved it, too. She used to decorate the house with pine boughs and ribbons and always had a pot of spices simmering on the stove."

"It sounds lovely."

"It was." He cocked his head to one side. "You could do the same, you know. The house is your home now. You can do with it what you want."

"You don't think Matthew would mind if I made changes?"

"No. I'm sure he wants you to feel at home, so do what you like."

Abe walked out of the stall and Julia petted the horse on the nose one last time before exiting as well. She shut the gate and lifted the rope back over the post to secure it and laid the brush down. When she turned around, Abe was gone. "Hello?" She turned a circle and didn't see him anywhere. "Abe?"

She stared around the barn for long minutes, wondering where he'd gone so fast. When he never came back, she shook her head at his quick disappearance. He'd done the same thing the day before.

Matthew and the other two ranch hands didn't return either so she let herself out of the barn and spotted them by one of the smaller buildings. Assuming her tour was over, she headed back to the house.

It was quiet when she entered. She hung her cloak and walked to the sitting room, taking note of all the things she'd like to change. Would Matthew mind? She bit her bottom lip, picturing the room with new curtains, the furniture rearranged to make the conversation area more inviting to guests—assuming they ever had any—by turning the fireplace into the focal point of the room. She may not be a great cook but she had great taste and it would take very little to spruce this place up. Then, once they were closer to Christmas, she'd decorate and make this the best holiday season her new husband had ever seen.

CHAPTER FIVE

The universe had finally put an end to his good fortune.

Over the past several weeks, he and Julia had fallen into a nice routine and each day gave him another small glimpse into the character of the woman he'd married. She'd fixed him a breakfast fit for a king earlier that morning, telling him it had been exactly four weeks since they married, then stared at him as if expecting a response, but he had no clue what she wanted to hear. His inability to talk to women had reared its head again and he'd left the house feeling like he'd done something wrong. The crestfallen look on Julia's face said he had, too.

The feeling had damn near ruined his whole day and now, he had to deal with this.

The gruesome display Matt saw splashed across the snow brought back a conversation he'd had with Levi Jackson weeks ago. The idle small talk the men who'd sent away for mail-order brides had while waiting for them to arrive at the church had ranged in topics, one of which was the wolves in the area. They were giving a few others in neighboring farms and ranches trouble but he'd not seen any sign of them before today. Now, it seemed as if they'd found his winter pasture.

One of the smaller cows had been attacked. The parts of it that hadn't been consumed or carried off had frozen and painted the hillside red.

Tracks in the snow showed more than one creature had been there. They were too close together to tell what exactly they were but if he had to guess, he'd say wolves. "We'll have to move the cattle closer to the house. This is too far away to be riding out and checking daily so tomorrow, we'll round up everyone else and herd them back in."

Silas and Orin nodded in agreement and turned their horses back to the house. The sun was low in the sky and as tired as he was, it took nothing more than a single thought of Julia waiting for him to make him push the horse faster.

Bright light shined from in windows when they made it back into the barnyard. He saw to his horse, wished Silas and Orin a good night and headed to the house.

He stepped up on the porch and looked into the window, seeing Julia cross the room to the sink before heading back to the table. His gaze was drawn to the way her hips swung from side to side as she walked and he cursed himself for being such a fool.

Those early days after they'd been married seemed so far away now and he'd yet to make her his wife all proper like. Lord knew he wanted to. He ached with the need to do so but she'd not given him any hint that she was ready. All she ever gave him was small coy smiles and even those drove him to distraction. He stood at the bottom of the stairs, night after night, willing himself to go up but he never did, reminding himself instead that she'd let him know when she was ready for him to come to her bed.

The smell of fresh bread filled the air when he stepped inside the house. As she'd done every night for weeks now, she graced him with a smile big enough to show him that dimple in her cheek and asked him if he was hungry. And every night, he felt his heart skip a beat as he looked at her and replied, "Yes, I'm starving."

He hung his hat and coat and went to the sink to wash up. By the time he'd dried his hands and turned to the table, Julia was setting out the food.

The first thing he noticed when he sat down was, the biscuits weren't burnt. The second was, she'd fixed enough to feed him three times over but as hungry as he was, he didn't have any doubts there would be leftovers.

She filled his plate before he could reach for it and he waited until she'd filled her own and sat down before picking up his fork. "Smells good." He picked up one of the biscuits. "I think you've finally gotten used to that old stove. You've not burned a biscuit in over two weeks."

Her cheeks turned a pretty shade of pink. "I'm sorry, I—"

"It's fine. They were edible."

"Barely."

He grinned at her embarrassment, then dug into his food. They ate in silence for long minutes before Julia said, "Do you mind if I make a few changes around the house?"

"No. This is your house now. Do with it what you wish."

"It won't be much. I'd like to move some of the furniture and maybe change the curtains. I shipped a number of things in those trunks I had sent out here and I'd like to put them to use."

She told him of all her plans and by the time they'd finished eating, he was positive there wasn't a sweeter sound in all of Montana than the soft cadence of her voice. He could have listened to it all night and wondered what it would sound like as he loved her. When she was panting for breath, clinging to him, and asking for more.

He shook himself from those thoughts and stood to clear away the dishes. She had water heating to wash them and when she tried to carry it over to the sink, he grabbed the bucket handle, his callused fingers brushing her hand as he did. "You cooked, let me clean up the mess."

Her eyes widened and her tongue darted out to wet her lips.

His gaze was drawn there and held, only her saying, "You wish to wash the dishes?" enough to make him look away.

He shrugged. "I'd been doing it for years before you arrived. Besides, you were the one who had to stand in here and cook. The least I can do is clean up the mess left behind." He thought she was going to refuse but finally nodded her head and let go of the bucket handle.

"Very well, then. Thank you."

He carried the bucket to the cabinet and poured the water into the wash tub as Julia told him she was going up to wash and get ready for bed. The moment she left the room, visions of her undressing, all that creamy ivory skin unveiled, filled his mind's eye. He wanted her in an instant. He wanted to climb those steps, strip down to nothing and crawl into that big bed with her, pull her close until they were skin to skin and taste her lips to see if they were as sweet as he imagined they were. He wanted to run his fingers through her hair, inhale the scent on her skin and feel her hands on him in places that hadn't been touched in years.

His body responded to the images running through his mind and he groaned, then looked to the ceiling. He had every right to climb those stairs and no one in Angel Creek would think poorly of him if he did. Julia was his wife and even though he'd told Pru he didn't want one, he was glad she'd gone behind his back and sent away for one anyway. He wasn't sure he would feel the same way if it were someone besides Julia in his upstairs bedroom, but it didn't matter now. She was his and as her husband, he had every right to sleep in her bed.

When he heard something scrape across the floor, his body tensed, images of her naked flesh being exposed filling his head again as he grabbed the first dish to give it a wash.

She brushed her hair one hundred times, rubbed the expensive body cream her father had given her for her last birthday onto her skin and put her nearly-see-through nightgown on and crawled into bed.

Fluffing the pillows behind her, she smoothed the blankets down over her hips and waited as she'd done for countless weeks now. Tonight would be different from all the others, she just knew it. She'd not missed the way Matthew had looked at her during supper or the way his eyes took on that darker shade of blue when she said she was going to get ready for bed. His gaze had landed on her mouth and stayed there and she wondered if he'd wanted to kiss her. Her heart fluttered at the thought.

She'd never been kissed. She was one of the few girls she knew that hadn't been. It wasn't that she'd never wanted a boy to kiss her, she just never let anyone know who she fancied, certainly not the boy she'd been pining for. She would have died of humiliation and knowing the vicious way some ladies in Charleston behaved, she had no doubt they'd tell half the town and find great pleasure in her mortification.

The house was quiet and she wondered what Matthew was doing. Was he still washing dishes? She had a hard time believing he'd want to do them—she'd never met a man who did woman's work—but was glad he'd volunteered. It meant he cared. Or she hoped it did. Prudence had told her she could tell Matthew liked her so she'd trust in that and hope for the best.

The chimes on the downstairs clock rang nine times and she looked at the bedroom door. How long had she been sitting there? She blew out a breath. Matthew wasn't coming to bed. The longer she sat there staring at the door, the more painful that ache in her heart grew. Reaching over to extinguish the lamp, she slid down into the bed and pulled the covers to her neck and ignored the sting of hot tears burning at her eyes.

It was obvious to her now that Matthew didn't want to consummate their marriage, but why? Did he not find her attractive? The thought made her heart clench. No one had ever wanted her. Too-tall Julia, as the kids called her, was still the ugly duckling and probably always would be. Those looks she thought she'd seen from him were nothing more than wishful thinking on her part and as the first tear fell, she realized that, despite her feelings for Matthew, she may be doomed to a loveless marriage.

CHAPTER SIX

They had a visitor. The man who'd ridden across the bridge on horseback was talking with Matthew and Silas. Julia stood watching them for several long minutes and it wasn't until Matthew and a few of the ranch hands climbed onto their horses and turned toward the pasture that she saw the shiny badge on the man's chest. The sheriff of Angel Creek—Sarah's new husband.

She hadn't seen her friends in so long and hoped when they came back from wherever they'd ridden off to, she'd have a chance to talk to him. She missed the others and wanted to visit them desperately. There were so many things to ask them. Sharing intimate details about her life wasn't something she'd ever thought she'd do but Matthew ignoring her wasn't normal. Or she didn't think so. They'd know if it was or not and would be able to advise her on what to do about it but the thought embarrassed her. Letting them know something was wrong would be humiliating but she couldn't go on like this. It was disheartening, and as the days wore on, she was almost convinced Matthew was hiding something from her. He was too—reserved. Quiet when she asked about his life before she arrived and the uneasiness that had settled in with his refusal to come to her bed intensified with every awkward conversation.

A quick inspection of the room left her feeling pleased. It looked inviting now and she straightened the crocheted lace doily she'd made and placed on the small table between the chairs. The furniture had been moved, the pieces situated the way she liked and she'd replaced those dark curtains, the room now bright and cheery.

The basket of dirty clothes she'd gathered before spotting the sheriff was still at the foot of the stairs. She picked it up and headed toward the kitchen, setting the basket down. When she opened the door to grab the wash tub, someone banged on the front door and she nearly jumped out of her skin.

Her heart was pounding as she hurried across the house, then skipped a beat when the thought of Sarah being there entered her mind. Had she come with the sheriff?

Running the rest of the way to the sitting room, the smile on her face so wide her cheeks were hurting as she pulled the front door open—and found Cora on the other side of it.

She let out a breath and kept her smile in place despite her disappointment. "Good morning." A look over the woman's shoulder showed her nothing other than a small sleigh and a man standing beside it. Julia had no idea who he was but if she had to guess, she'd say he was nothing more than an escort.

Turning her attention back to Cora, their first encounter was once again fresh on her mind. She hadn't missed the animosity between her and Prudence, nor had she been able to ignore the sneer that had been thrown her way, but despite her first impression of her, Julia took a step back and said, "Would you like to come in?"

Cora swept into the room with a swish of skirts and turned a full circle when she got to the middle of the room. Julia closed the door and faced her. "It's nice to see you again, Cora."

"I'm here to speak with Matthew."

The same disdainful look Cora had given her in town was thrown her way again and for the second time, Julia felt as if she wasn't privy to some important piece of information. "I'm afraid he isn't here."

"What time do you expect him back?"

"I don't know. He and the sheriff left not long ago. They rode toward the pasture behind the barn. I'm not sure how long they'll be."

Cora looked around the room again, then untied her cloak. "I'll wait."

Julia took her cloak and hung it by the door as Cora made herself at home. She'd dealt with more than one young lady who wasn't pleasant to be around and Cora was turning into one very quickly. "Could I offer you some coffee?"

"I prefer tea."

Who didn't? She forced another smile onto her face. "As do I, but we're out at the moment." She didn't mention that there had never been any to begin with.

Cora sighed heavily, her head turning from left to right. "You've moved the furniture."

"Yes. It was too spread out before. You won't have to yell to be heard with the chairs closer together like this."

"It was fine before." She glanced at the windows and squinted before putting her back to them. "Those curtain's let too much light in. In the summer, the sun shines directly in those windows and heats this part of the house until it's nearly unbearable." She met her gaze and cocked her head to one side. "Did Matthew tell you to change them?"

"No."

"I didn't think so. He prefers the curtains dark to block the light."

"Oh. Well, he's not said anything about me changing them."

"I don't suppose he would."

Something in the way Cora was looking at her, and the quiet

scornfulness of her words, were enough to make her wary. As pleasant as Cora had been when first meeting her, she certainly didn't act as if she liked her now.

She didn't owe anyone any explanations for her actions but found herself saying, "Matthew and I talked about the changes I wanted to make. He had no problem with anything I wished to do as this is now my home as well as his."

If one could come to harm from looks alone, she was sure she would have been frozen where she stood by the glacial stare Cora was giving her and honestly, her hospitality would only extend so far. "Have I done something to offend you, Cora?"

A muscle ticked in the woman's cheek. "Since you've asked, yes, you have."

Julia moved to the sofa and braced her hands on the back of it. "Then, my apologies. Whatever it is, I can assure you I meant no offense."

"Your apology does me little good now that you've married my fiancé."

The words shook her to her core. Julia stared at Cora, her heart racing in her chest, the words, Matthew was Cora's fiancé, ringing inside her head. Their exchange inside Thompson's now made more sense. Cora had been pleasant until she mentioned she was Matthew's wife. The look on her face had changed instantly and once Prudence came inside and referred to her as her sister-in-law, Cora had turned hostile. At least now she knew why.

She rounded the end of the sofa on wobbly legs and sat down. "I wasn't aware there was an arrangement between you and Matthew, Cora. Had I known, I assure you, I wouldn't have made the trip out here and I certainly wouldn't have married your fiancé."

"Well, you can thank Prudence for that. She's meddled in Matthew's affairs his entire life, sending away for you only being the latest."

"Sending away for me?"

Cora smiled but she didn't think there was anything friendly about the gesture "Oh, you didn't know?" The smug look on her face turned triumphant. "Matthew didn't send away for a new bride, Julia. Why would he? Prudence is the one who sent for you. She went behind his back and never told him." Before she could ask Cora why Prudence would do such a thing, she said, "She's never liked me and she knew Matthew and I would marry next year. Sending away for you was her way of making sure that never happened. That, and to spite me."

"I see." So many things made sense now and the heaviness she'd felt in her chest seemed to grow as she sat there staring at Cora—the woman her husband loved enough to want to marry. She felt miserable in an instant. Matthew had a fiancé—was in love with Cora—and had been making plans to marry her. No wonder he hadn't bothered coming to her bed. He didn't want her. He never had and never would.

Cora stood abruptly, the look in her eyes different from what it had been. She looked almost—happy now. "I just remembered another appointment I have this morning and can't wait any longer. Tell Matthew I wish to speak to him." She walked to the door and grabbed her cloak, wrapping it around her shoulders. "Will you be coming to the Christmas party?"

It took every ounce of willpower she had to speak without her voice trembling. "I haven't received an invitation to a party."

"Oh, well invitations are rarely sent. It's not so formal as that. The party is held annually and is the highlight of the year here in Angel Creek." Pulling the hood on her cloak up over her head, she said, "Be sure to let Matthew know how much you want to go."

That funny look entered Cora's eyes again before she gave her a smirk and left. She was out the door before Julia had time to ask why it was important for her to be there. She managed to make it to the window without her knees buckling and peeked out at her. The man she'd seen earlier was helping Cora into the sleigh, then he climbed in himself, before turning the sleigh around and headed toward the bridge.

"I'd stay away from that one if I were you."

Julia jumped, a scream lodged in her throat at the sound of Abe's voice right behind her. She glanced over her shoulder and saw him leaning back against the chair Cora had been sitting in. "Please stop sneaking up on me."

He grinned. "I can't help myself. I used to hide and jump out to scare Pru when she was younger. Even managed to make her pee herself a time or two."

"How awful."

He laughed. "Nah, just good fun. Besides, she started it. She thought scaring an old man was the funniest thing in the world so, we made a game of it. She outgrew it. I did not."

"Obviously. I knew your sudden appearances weren't because I wasn't paying attention." Despite her mood, Julia gave him a tiny smile. "You've just mastered the ability to sneak up on me without me hearing you."

He motioned out the window to the retreating sleigh. "Don't let that one get you down. She spits more venom than any other person I ever met. She was always a testy little thing and now it looks as if that pretty smile on her face hides a shrewd woman. My Pru sees right through her though. Matthew on the other hand, does not. He only sees the good in people, regardless of how little there may be of it."

And Matthew's good nature is why her last name was now Bailey and Cora's wasn't. He'd shown up at that church and married her because his sister sent away for her, and being the man he is, he didn't refuse the promise Prudence made on his behalf.

"I like the new curtains." He nodded as he took in the room. "Those old drab ones that were in here made the place resemble a tomb more than a home. It looks as if someone lives here again.

Now, all it needs is a bit of cheering up." That mischievous smile returned to his face. "It won't be long until Christmas. What say we spruce this place up a bit?"

The mention of Christmas pushed all the dark thoughts from Julia's head in an instant. "I love Christmas."

"It used to be a big deal around here. Not so much anymore but now that you're here, I think it's time to shake things up." He pointed to the corner next to the fireplace. "The tree used to sit in that corner. It always looked nice there. I say you put a big one up and fill this place with as much Christmas cheer as it can hold."

Julia stared at the corner and imagined a tree there. It certainly would make it feel more like Christmas but with Cora's revelations, she wasn't sure she should be trying to celebrate.

"You're thinking too much." He walked to the door and hooked a thumb toward it. "Go out there and find Orin and have him take you to get a tree."

"Are you sure I should?"

"Why shouldn't you?"

She shrugged.

"If Matt didn't want to marry you, he wouldn't have."

"But Cora—"

"—Has always wished for something that wasn't there. Now stop worrying and go get a tree."

Finding the perfect tree wasn't as simple as she thought it would be. They'd walked what seemed like hours by the creek bank, picking tree after tree, Orin getting ready to hack it down before she'd see another she liked better. The moment Orin started to chop it down, another one caught her eye.

"Wait. I want that one instead." Julia grinned when Orin raised an eyebrow at her. "Are you sure?"

She laughed and nodded her head. "Yes, I'm positive. I truly like that one. I promise this time."

Orin tossed the hatchet into the air, end over end, before catching the handle and bending over at the tree, chopping it down before she could stop him again. He straightened when it fell, grabbed hold of the base and grinned. "Let's go before you see another you like better."

They walked back in silence. Once in the house, he was unusually quiet as he helped her set it up. When it was secure and they were both sure it wouldn't fall over, he stared at it for long moments before giving her a peculiar look.

"What is it?"

He scratched his chin. "Nothing."

"That wasn't a nothing look. You've been acting strange since I asked you to help me cut the tree down."

He blew out a breath. "Does Matt know about this?"

"The tree?"

"Yeah."

"No, not yet, but he'll see it once he comes in. Why?"

He gave her a side-eyed look then shook his head. "I'm sure it'll be fine."

"Why wouldn't it be?"

He opened his mouth to say something but closed it and shrugged his shoulders. "Anything else I can do for you?"

Julia shook her head no and thanked him, then followed him outside. The sun was shining, the glare off the snow near blinding and she squinted and stared in the direction of the barn. Matthew and the sheriff rode back over the hill, two ranch hands close behind them.

She lifted a hand to shield her eyes from the sun as they dismounted, Matthew pulling a long-barreled gun from a holster on the horse's saddle. The sheriff said something, then turned and left as quickly as he'd come. Her shoulders drooped with her disappointment. She'd wanted to speak to him, to ask about Sarah and the others.

Silas grabbed the reins on Matthew's horse and took him inside the barn, her husband readjusting his hat and following him inside without a single glance her way.

She sighed as she watched him disappear inside the building. Cora's visit was still fresh on her mind. It had been since the woman left and it didn't take much to start thinking that her being there was a mistake. The fact she was still as virginal as she'd been when she arrived was telling. She'd been Matthew's wife long enough for things to have progressed further than they had and now she knew why they hadn't.

All those looks she thought she'd seen him give her? Nothing but her imagination.

The wind gusted and she shivered and walked back inside. The fire was blazing and she held her hands out to warm them as she stared at the tree. It looked a bit lonely and out of place.

From behind her, Abe said, "It needs decorations."

Julia screamed at the sound of his voice and spun around on her heel, hand to her heart. Abe was standing behind her, arms crossed over his chest, head cocked to one side as he stared at the tree.

"Don't do that!"

He chuckled. "You are a skittish little thing."

She took deep breaths to try and calm her racing heart and tried to be angry at him but the grin on his face made it hard to be. "I've never been called little in my life. I'm too tall for that distinction and I'm not skittish. I just didn't hear you come in is all. You startled me—again."

He ran his gaze over her from head to toe. "I suppose you are tall for a woman. Nothing wrong with it. My Ester was tall, too. You remind me a lot of her, you know."

"Do I?"

He nodded and looked around the room. "You plan on decorating the whole house or just this room?"

"I don't know. I hadn't thought much further than the tree."

"Out in the thicket that tree came from you'll find a few smaller trees perfect for pine boughs. Some of those bushes still have the dried-up husks of berries on them. My Ester always brought those inside as well. They'll make the house smell good too but if you put them near the mantle, you'll have to replace them before Christmas. They'll dry out that close to the fire and the needles will drop right off."

"Oh, right. I hadn't thought of that. My father always took care of all of the particulars. He always found enormous Christmas trees for the house and had someone come in to decorate every year. It was always so grand and the house smelled wonderful." She sighed. "Father always hosted a party. This is the first year I'll miss it."

"Hold your own."

She grinned. "I don't think I'm up for hosting a party. It's too late to even plan one, anyway. Besides, there's a big party being held in town. I'm sure everyone will be there."

"Will you?"

She shrugged. "I don't know. Matthew hasn't mentioned it and I only found out about it today."

"Well, bring it up. He needs some time away from this ranch. He worries too much."

Julia raised her head at that. "Worried about what?"

"Nothing for you to be concerned about." He smiled and nodded to the door. "Best go get those pine boughs. Matt will be in hunting his lunch before too long."

"I suppose you're right." She glanced at the clock and went to the back door to grab her cloak. When she returned, Abe was gone. "What in the—"

She peeked into the other room and saw nothing. She blew out a breath. "For an old man, you sure are quick on your feet."

Heading to the fireplace, she stirred the coals in the fire so it wasn't blazing then grabbed the large basket by the door and headed out.

As luck would have it, Orin had left the hatchet on the porch. She'd not have to pull or break off any limbs she found. Placing it in her basket, she headed for the same grove of trees he'd taken her to not half an hour earlier.

Her booted feet made a soft crunching sound as she stepped underneath the trees. The snow had frozen over here and a thin layer of ice had formed.

Finding the bush with small red berries she assumed Abe had been talking about, she set down the basket, grabbed the hatchet and began cutting off the smallest limbs. She made a mental list of where she'd place them in the house as she put the first small limb into her basket and hoped she remembered to check the larder to see what sort of spices Matthew had. She could simmer a few on the stove and fill the house with the same fragrant scents she was used to at Christmas.

She'd broken a good sweat when she heard the snow behind her crunching. She finished cutting off the limb she was hacking on and tossed it into her basket before turning around. Then froze.

The weeks of preparation to come to Montana had been spent going through every book she could find on the sort of wildlife she may encounter here and the wolf was one she hoped never to come across. The one standing in front of her looked as terrifying as those she'd read about and when his lip curled up to reveal his teeth, her heart skipped a beat.

His growl started low then grew in volume and when he took a small step toward her, she took one backward, her entire body seeming to start rattling all at once. Her limbs grew shaky, her heart raced and she gripped the hatchet handle tightly and took another step backward.

The wolf lowered its head and Julia flicked a quick glance

toward the house. She could barely make it out through the trees. Would the wolf attack if she ran?

He growled, the sound a low rumble, and tears instantly stung the back of her eyes. She blinked them away, lifting the hatchet a few inches. "Please go away." She kept her voice soft, barely over a whisper. "Don't make me use this. I have no desire to kill an animal." *Or be eaten by one.*

The wolf tore his yellow gaze from her for a brief second and looked to its left. Julia did the same and saw another wolf stalking in close. Her heart started pounding, blood rushing to her head so quickly she felt dizzy as images of them attacking her filled her mind. The wolf took another step toward her and she lifted the hatchet, gripped the handle with both hands and took slow steps to the side, trying to make a wide circle around the thing in order to head back to the house.

She'd taken less than a dozen steps when he jumped. Julia's heart lodged in her throat and she screamed until her lungs felt as if they would burst and swung the hatchet when the animal was inches from her face. They both hit the ground, the wolf stunned from the blow she'd given it and she scrambled away on all fours, screaming when the other wolf sprang for her.

Raising the hatchet, she swung at it, clipping it on the nose and felt something warm splatter across her face. She hurried to her feet, gripped the hatchet with two hands again and tried to see through her tears. "Stay where you are," she said, sniffling. The first wolf was bleeding from a large cut next to its ear, the other, its nose, both of their injuries staining the snow red. When the wolf with the cut ear lunged for her a second time, she prayed they didn't kill her.

Julia was screaming.

Matt ran for the house, rifle in hand, his blood freezing in his veins. He heard shouts behind him, the other ranch hands reacting to her screams as well, and it only took seconds to hear them running after him.

Footprints led from the house into the copse of trees near the creek. Another scream, followed by what sounded like an animal, had him lifting the gun as he churned up snow and raced for the trees.

He saw them the moment he stepped under the canopy of limbs. Julia was on the ground, a wolf laying a few feet away from her. When it stood, and she began to crawl away, his heart lodged in his throat as both wolves lunged for her.

The gunshot was deafening as he pulled the trigger. He didn't know if he'd hit either animal but they ran. He darted around the trees and saw blood on the ground when he was only a few feet away from her.

"Julia!"

"I'm all right," she said, rolling to her side and trying to sit up.

The wolves were gone by the time he reached her. He fell to one knee, laid the gun on the ground and helped her sit up, his hands skating across her bloody face and arms. He pulled his hands away, his fingers coated with blood. "Where did they bite you?"

"They didn't. I'm fine." She looked at his hands and shook her head. "It's not mine. I got one of them with the hatchet."

He looked over his shoulder to where the wolves had run and caught a glimpse of Orin chasing after them. Silas stopped by his side, winded. "How many of them did you see?"

"Only two," Matt said. Julia's eyes were wide, her breaths panted out and he wasn't sure who was shaking more—her or him. "Were there others, Julia?"

She took a deep breath and let it out before saying, "No. Two is all I saw but I wasn't looking for more. I was afraid to look away from the one in front of me."

He grabbed his rifle and handed it to Silas and motioned him in the direction Orin had gone, then helped Julia to stand. When her knees went out from under her, he scooped her off the ground.

"I can walk. Just give me a second."

He ignored her and headed back to the house, the screams echoing inside his head until that's all he heard. Julia made a small noise and he realized he was squeezing her to him and loosened his tight hold on her.

It took three tries to grab the door handle and he ended up kicking the door in his haste to open it, Julia jumping in his arms at the sound. He sat her on the sofa, helped her remove the cloak then inspected every inch of her that he dared, ignoring her when she continued to say she was fine. He took her cloak and stood, pacing away, willing his hands to stop shaking as he draped it over the arm of the chair. His thoughts were racing, her screams joining those that haunted him daily, and only the look on Julia's face brought him back to her side. He knelt in front of her and when he was sure he could speak without his voice trembling, he said, "What were you doing out there?"

"Collecting pine boughs."

"Pine boughs?" His confusion must have shown on his face because she said, "I wanted them for decorations," before he could ask why she needed them.

He looked around the room and spotted the tree. That Christmas all those years ago filled his mind's eye the instant he saw it. The house had been filled with festive decorations then. Pru had insisted they be put up, even though it was only him and his pa living there. He'd ripped them down that day, burned them all and hadn't acknowledged Christmas since. Knowing Julia nearly died not two weeks before that anniversary sent white-hot fury racing through his veins.

"Where the hell did that come from?"

She glanced in the direction of the tree and hesitated before saying, "Orin helped me bring it in."

Memories by the dozens came flooding back the longer he stared at it, the screams echoing inside his head again. He was shaking as he crossed the room to grab the tree. He hauled it to the front door and tossed it out, nearly hitting Orin and Silas as they neared the porch. Orin was carrying a basket, those pine boughs Julia had been collecting filling the inside and he was across the porch, snatching the basket from Orin's hand and tossing it away before anyone could say a word.

He pointed a trembling finger at Orin, his jaw clenching tight before saying, "Don't ever take my wife into the woods again, especially for something as useless as a tree."

"I'm sorry, Matt. I didn't mean—"

Matthew didn't let him finish and stormed back into the house. His heart was racing to the point he felt dizzy. Julia was where he'd left her, her eyes wide. "I don't want to see another tree in this house. Am I clear?" When she nodded her head at him, his gut churned as images of her torn into pieces like the young cow had been filled his head. "And don't go back into the woods. I don't need another death on my conscious. I have plenty as it is!"

She didn't say anything but didn't have to. The fear on her face as she lowered her head to stare at her hands said enough. If he hadn't been so furious, he would have probably felt bad for the tears in her eyes, and for yelling at her but, at the moment, all he could see was her in the blood-covered snow staring lifelessly at nothing.

He stared at her until his heart resumed a normal beat and opened his mouth to say, what he had no idea, but closed it without uttering a word. *You almost lost her.* The thought whispered across his mind and in an instant he was mad all over again. Those wolves needed to be dealt with.

He stormed out of the house, slamming the door shut behind him and hurried back across the barnyard, Silas and Orin following along quietly. He was still shaking when he walked inside the barn, his eyes taking several minutes to adjust to the dim interior.

Orin looked much like Julia did when he turned to face him, the only difference being he wasn't crying, but the remorse on his face was plain to see. He bit back more words he'd regret later and hurried to the stall his horse was in and started to saddle him.

Silas cleared his throat. "Is Mrs. Bailey all right?"

He didn't answer right away, deciding to wait until he'd calmed a bit. When he knew he could talk to them without yelling he nodded his head. "Yes. She's shaken up but other than that, I think she's fine. She wasn't hurt."

He tightened the last cinch and guided the horse out of the stall, then looked at Silas. "Go 'round up the others. If those wolves are still on my property, I want them dead." Silas nodded and turned on his heel. When Orin turned to follow him, Matt stopped him. "I want you to stay near the house and keep an eye on Julia. Make sure she doesn't go out into those woods again."

Orin promised to not let her out of his sight and followed him out of the barn. When Matt climbed into his saddle, he gave a quick glance to the house before taking off toward town, the scene in the woods replaying in his head on repeat with every step the horse made.

The sight of her face splattered with blood wouldn't leave him, nor would the vision of her laying in the snow surrounded by large swaths of it. It hadn't been hers but it could have been. Had he been a few minutes later in reaching her, all that blood could have been hers.

It took longer than it should have for him to finally calm down, the small trails of smoke in the distance from the houses in town coming into view before the screams inside his head faded. He ran a hand down his face and released a pent-up breath. What if he'd reached her too late? What if he'd not been fast enough and he'd lost her? She'd only been his for a short time and the thought of her not being there made him realize how much he wanted her. How much he wanted to hold her close.

Seeing her there on the couch covered in blood splatters with tears pooling in her eyes filled him with the desire to grab her, to pull her to him and not let go but he wasn't sure such intimacy would have been welcomed. She'd made no mention of him coming to her bed so he doubted she wanted that sort of attention from him. She wasn't ready for their relationship to progress to that point or she would have let him know. Wouldn't she?

Or was she waiting on him?

He blew out a breath. Surely she knew how much he wanted to be a proper husband to her. What man wouldn't? Especially when his wife was as lovely as Julia was.

You should have told her. Maybe she's waiting for you.

His thoughts ran in circles as he rode closer to town. Something needed to change. They couldn't go on being strangers. He didn't want to. He wanted his wife. Wanted to be a proper husband to her and once he got home, he'd see about making that happen. Right now, he needed to speak with the sheriff. Those wolves needed to be dealt with and quickly. His wife's life may depend on it.

CHAPTER SEVEN

When the front door slammed shut, the tears Julia was holding back fell unbidden. She was near blind from them when she jumped from the sofa and ran for the stairs and up to her room.

From her window, she saw Matthew on his horse, galloping across the bridge and seeing him broke her heart all over again, the torrent of tears erupting as she sobbed.

She staggered to the bed, tears blinding her as she sat down. She'd never been yelled at. Her father had spoiled her and he'd never raised his voice with her until she'd told him she was leaving for Montana but he'd apologized immediately and hugged her close until she believed he was truly sorry.

But Matthew hadn't done that. He'd yelled, his anger apparent with every harsh word he spoke, and now her heart hurt, the pain so intense it felt as if it were going to crumble inside her chest.

She cried for long minutes, her heart bleeding out until the pain was a physical ache. She'd never feared Matthew, not once since arriving and if anyone had reason to fear another it was her. They were strangers after all, and even though he seemed pleasant enough, it didn't mean he was.

Had she been wrong about him after all this time? Was he

prone to violent rages? She'd heard of many men who possessed bad tempers they couldn't control and almost all of them were prone to strike whether the object of their anger was male or female. Would Matthew strike her? She hadn't thought so until today.

She crossed to the water pitcher and bowl and wet one of the small hand towels there and washed her face, laying the cool cloth to her red eyes before venturing back downstairs when the signs of her crying fit were gone.

The door was cracked open. It must not have latched when Matthew slammed it. She went to close it but stopped when she saw the tree lying next to the porch. Why had he reacted so violently when he saw it? It had been tucked into the corner, out of the way. It would have hurt nothing for it to be there.

She shut the door and turned, not at all surprised to see Abe standing next to the fireplace. For once he didn't startle a scream out of her and he said nothing until she gave him a tiny, forced smile.

"He didn't mean to yell at you like that. He was just scared is all." His voice was pitched low, the soothing tone comforting. "We men don't know how else to deal with an emotion like fear other than yelling. It's that or hit something and I reckon that would have frightened you more than the yelling did."

"He couldn't have been nearly as frightened as me."

"Oh, I imagine he was."

She met his gaze, and for once, saw no laughter dancing in his blue eyes.

He motioned to one of the chairs and said, "Sit down. Your face looks as white as my hair."

Her mouth tilted up on one end, a smile trying to form as she did what he said. They didn't speak for a long time, the only sound to be heard that of the clock on the mantle. When he continued to stand there and stare at her, she sighed. "Do you know why he reacted that way?"

He nodded. "I do, but it's not my story to tell. Matt has issues with this time of year. He and Pru both do. Christmas isn't joyful for either of them and when they're ready to tell you why, they will, but just know Matthew cares about you whether he shows it or not and I'm sure he's beating himself up over the way he reacted."

"How can you know that?"

"Know what?"

"That he cares for me?"

"A man can tell when another is sweet on his wife."

She doubted Matthew held any affection for her. Most days he acted as if he barely realized she was there, and other than the few times he'd carried her for one reason or another and holding her hands at the church when they married, he hadn't touched her. "I don't think Matthew holds any ill will toward me but I don't think he's sweet on me in the least. He tolerates me, I think, and the longer I'm here, the more I wonder if I made a mistake coming to Montana."

"Now don't be thinking like that. I can tell you for a fact he's head over heels for ya. I've known him since the day he came squalling into this world and I've been around him long enough to read every expression on his face. He cares for you, Julia, he just has a poor way of showing it. Most men do."

He moved closer to where she sat and gave her a smile. "Don't lose faith him in, girl. The things he's had to deal with are enough to break most folk but he's still here and trying and I'm sure he'll come home sorrier than he's ever been in his life."

He headed to the kitchen and Julia leaned back in her chair and blew out a breath. She wasn't sure she believed everything Abe said but the notion of going home wouldn't leave her thoughts. Doing so would require sending word to her father for funds to make the trip and how would she tell her friends? Leaving them would be painful, but leaving Matthew would be unbearable. Despite his inattention to her, her heart fluttered every time he walked into the room. She'd never been in love but she'd been sweet on enough young gentlemen to know what she felt for Matthew was unlike anything she'd ever experienced before. Leaving would break her heart but if what Cora said was true, staying was pointless because no matter how much she willed it so, Matthew would never love her.

Someone had decorated the town. Pine boughs filled every window, ribbons and candles adorning them, and every person he saw had a smile on their face. That, along with the constant snow flurries, brought back so many memories he wasn't sure how he survived them anymore. The pain was still raw, even after all these years.

Seeing that tree in the house had felt like a punch to his gut, as if the universe was in constant need to remind him how he'd failed his family, and inadvertently, caused their deaths. His reaction to seeing it had been fueled by raw pain but it paled in comparison to seeing that look of fear on Julia's face. Her tears made that wound he's never been able to heal split wide open again.

He should have never yelled at her. He should have walked away and calmed down but the thought of those wolves tearing into her had put a fear into him unlike anything else ever had. He'd been so close to losing her.

Thinking of those wolves made the anger return and every harsh word he'd spoken to Julia echoed inside his head again. He knew he had to make things right between them but he didn't know how. Words seemed useless but he owed her an explanation, even though the thought of telling that story made him sick to his stomach. He'd do what he had to do to make things right, but first, he had to tell the sheriff about those wolves showing up again.

Quinn's office was dark when he stopped in front of it. He turned to look down the street in the direction of his house. He didn't want to bother him at home, so he let himself into the office and left a note on the desk for him. Knowing Quinn, he'd be by to check on things before he turned in for the night anyway and really, beyond telling him what happened, there wasn't anything the sheriff could do other than let the nearby ranchers know what had happened. Julia had escaped unharmed but that didn't mean everyone would and the thought of someone else losing a loved one was unacceptable. He'd come back tomorrow after breakfast to make sure Quinn saw the note and ride to every ranch and farm on the prairie himself if he had to, to tell everyone personally to be on the lookout for that pack of wolves.

When he'd left, he crossed town to the mercantile. He had no idea how to apologize to Julia but most women liked gifts, so he looked at nearly everything the Weston's had on the many shelves and tables. He was about to give up when he spotted a shelf with decorative round tins, the labels on them printed with flowers and a foreign language.

He picked one up and removed the lid to peer inside of it.

"It's imported all the way from overseas."

Matt glanced at Cassie Weston as she stopped beside him. "Have you tried any of them?"

"Only one. I didn't care for it. I prefer coffee to tea." She cocked her head to one side. "But I can tell you those other ladies from down south sure do like them."

"Do they?"

"Yes. They've bought nearly all I had. Those four containers are all that's left until I can get more ordered. They're all different, too. Who knew tea came in such varieties."

Matt picked up every tin. The others would just have to wait for more. "I'll take them all, then."

Cassie smiled and pointed to a tea service on the next shelf over, the white teapot and cups adorned with dark pink flowers and green vines. Small saucers and plates trimmed in the same dark pink color fit perfectly on a white tray.

"If she makes her tea in your coffee pot, she'll more than likely taste coffee and not the tea."

The price tag on the set was laughable but after the way he'd treated his new bride, he would have paid double. He nodded and said, "I'll take it."

Cassie's eyes widened. She'd clearly not believed the mere mention of the set would be enough to sell it and he knew from now on, she'd try to hand-sell him everything in the store.

He followed her to the counter and paid, nodding to Mrs. Peterson as she walked up to the counter and was watching Cassie wrap each piece of the tea service when the bell above the door rang. They both looked up. Seeing Cora standing there staring at him was the perfect ending to an already disastrous day.

She turned on her heel and rushed back outside, the door slamming in her wake.

Matt blew out a breath and said, "I'll be back for that in a few minutes, Cassie," before heading across the store and out the door. As much as he'd dreaded the thought of talking to Cora, it was time to set things right.

CHAPTER EIGHT

It was obvious the happy laughter she'd spent years enjoying at Christmas weren't to be this year. Julia turned away from the window and sat down. Staring at the tree Matthew had tossed outside only made her more miserable, and for the first time since arriving, she was truly homesick for everything she'd left behind.

She missed her father and even Bess, cranky as she was at times, and longed for the familiar comforts of home and the sound of ocean waves lapping at the shore. She wanted to taste salt on the breeze again as the sea spray filled the air with the scents of the ocean.

She missed the parties and laughter and her friends.

She missed the warm hugs her father gave her.

She missed feeling wanted.

Julia stared into the fireplace, watching the flames dance across the logs as they popped and hissed, so lost in thought she didn't hear the door open until it shut. She sat up thinking it was Matthew but slumped back into her chair when she saw Prudence hanging her cloak up.

"Why is there a tree laying in the front yard?"

Looking back at the fire and blowing out a deep inhaled breath, Julia said, "Because Matthew didn't want it in the house."

Prudence was quiet for so long Julia thought maybe she'd left as quietly as Abe always seemed to do and turned her head to see. Prudence was still by the door, a peculiar look on her face. "What?"

"You brought a tree in?"

"Yes." Prudence acted as odd about the tree as Matthew had and it made little sense. Did they not celebrate Christmas in Montana as they did in South Carolina?

As she stared at Prudence, her conversation with Cora whispered back through her mind again and the question that had been tugging at her conscious ever since then reared its head. "Why did you send away for Matthew a bride?"

Prudence's head snapped up. "Who said I did?"

"Cora."

The sneer that crossed her face was all she needed to see to know Cora had been right about one thing. Those two did not get along. "Why do you dislike her so much?"

"Who said I did?"

"Your face."

Prudence snorted a laugh. "Fair enough." She crossed the room and sat down in the chair opposite Julia. "Cora is a spoiled daddy's girl who always gets what she wants. That store of theirs was built just for her and she's always had to be the best-dressed in town and has a hissy fit if anyone outshines her in any way. Call it jealousy if you'd like, but she's always rubbed me the wrong way, as she does many folks. I've never really liked her, especially after she set her sights on my brother when they were both in school and she was determined to have him. Lord knows she's gone out of her way to see that he was hers by any means possible."

Julia took in the new information and looked back at the fire. "Does Matthew love her?"

Prudence laughed loudly at that. "Heck no."

"Cora said they were engaged."

Prudence rolled her eyes. "I just bet she did." She shook her head and leaned forward in her seat. "Listen to me. Matt's a nice guy, he always has been, but he has never loved Cora, nor has he ever asked her to marry him."

"But Cora said—"

"—I can only imagine what Cora said." Prudence leaned back again and crossed her feet at the ankles. "Cora whined about never finding a suitable husband in a town as small as Angel Creek to anyone who would listen and my good-natured brother tried to reassure her she'd not end up a spinster. He made the mistake of teasingly telling her he'd marry her himself if she hadn't done so by her twenty-fifth birthday and the girl took it to heart. She's turned down every suitor who's come knocking on her door because of it. Whatever she told you, don't believe a word of it, because I can assure you, Matthew does not want her."

Julia wasn't so sure about that. "I don't think he wants me either."

"Nonsense." When she said nothing in return, Prudence said, "Is everything okay?"

Julia gave her a tiny smile and nodded her head. "Yes, everything is fine."

"Liar."

Prudence shifted in her seat moments before Julia saw her out of the corner of her eye. She was leaning forward, elbows propped on her knees.

"I can tell something is bothering you, Julia, so talk to me. I know we're practically strangers, and I'd never presume to be as close to you as those friends you traveled across the country with are, but I'd very much like to be considered your friend. You can talk to me about anything. I promise it won't leave this room."

Julia had wanted desperately to talk to Ruby and the others about her troubles but the more she thought about it, the more she realized they couldn't help her. They knew nothing about her husband—but Prudence did. She probably knew him better than anyone else in the entire town.

She sat up straight and stared at her hands. "I think I made a mistake in coming out here." For the third time that day, tears filled her eyes. She blinked them away. "I think it might be best if I went home."

Prudence's lips drew into a harsh line. "Stop talking nonsense. You are home."

"Then why do I feel like a guest?"

"I don't know. Why do you feel that way?"

She flicked a quick glance to Prudence's face before looking away.

The things she wanted to ask were so personal she would have had a hard time talking about them with her friends. Mentioning them to her husband's sister? Mortifying.

"Your face is turning red."

Julia laid her hands on her cheeks, heat crawling up her neck before burning her entire face. Just the thought of talking about intimate things with someone else was embarrassing.

"Wait a minute." Prudence slid to the edge of her chair. "When you said you didn't think Matthew wanted you, did you say it for a specific reason?"

Her face burned hotter.

"Lord have mercy." Prudence blew out a breath and mumbled something under her breath. "Has he—"

"—I don't think he wants to be married," Julia interrupted. "At least, not married to me."

"That's ridiculous, Julia. If Matt didn't want to marry you, he wouldn't have. He's a good guy but he's also pig-headed and strong-willed. He doesn't do anything he doesn't want to do. Trust me, if he married you, it's because he wanted to."

Cora was halfway down the street when Matthew stepped out onto the wooden sidewalk and he had to jog to catch up with her.

She darted into her family's store and he barely got his hand on the door before she slammed it shut. "May I come in, Cora?"

She was furious. Her face was red, her mouth set into a hard, straight line and the look in her eyes should have killed him where he stood. She narrowed her eyes, hissing, "Nothing you can say will make what you did all right!"

"And what did I do?"

Her jaw clenched. "You said you'd marry me, Matthew! That if I reached twenty-five and had not done so, that you'd marry me."

He sighed and rubbed a hand down his face. Shuffling footsteps to his left drew his attention. Cora's shouting had drawn onlookers.

"If you wish to talk this out, then open the door, otherwise I'm going home."

She sneered at him and said, "Back to her?"

"Open the door, Cora."

She looked like she was going to refuse but swung it open a moment later and stormed into the building, slinging her reticule onto a table filled with scarves.

Matt shut the door behind him and was quiet for long minutes as Cora paced the width of the building, her jaw locked tight. When she finally looked his way he said, "Prudence sent away for a bride." He cringed the moment the words were out of his mouth. "That's not an excuse, it's just the way it happened."

Cora laughed but there wasn't anything humorous in the sound. "I know she was the one who did it. Mrs. Peterson told me last week she'd overheard the entire conversation those men had about sending away for wives, and when she told me Prudence had been there, I knew she did it just to spite me."

Knowing Prudence, she probably did, but he didn't say as much out loud. "I didn't know anything about it until Julia's trunks arrived at the house. I was in the process of having them sent back, thinking it was a mistake when Pru showed up and told me I couldn't, that they weren't at the wrong address. That's the day she told me she'd sent away for a bride and that Julia would be there the following week so it was too late to send word for her not to come."

"But you showed up at the church—"

"—Only to tell her I couldn't marry her."

"Then why did you?"

Because she was the prettiest thing he'd ever seen. Because she took his breath away when she set those green eyes on him and smiled, and he'd felt like the luckiest man in the entire world when she crossed the room and took his outstretched hand.

But he wasn't about to tell Cora that.

He scratched at his beard. "She was hundreds of miles away from home, Cora. She was alone except for her friends, penniless for all I knew. What would have happened to her had I refused?"

She crossed her arms over her chest and turned her head to stare at anything but him.

"I couldn't leave her stranded here, Cora. It would have been cruel to promise her a home and marriage and then turn her away after she'd traveled half the country to get here."

"But you didn't promise her."

"No, but my name was on that request, and to Julia, it was me who sent for her. She still thinks I sent away for her."

Her head snapped back around and her mouth opened as if she was about to say something but she closed it with a snap.

"What?"

"Nothing."

He shoved his hands into his coat pockets. "I did what I thought was the decent thing to do, Cora. I know you've been turning down suitors." To her credit, she blushed. "And I know you've been holding out in hopes we'd marry—"

"Would you have?"

Not by choice.

"Had Julia not shown up, would you have married me?"

"I'm a man of my word, Cora."

Her shoulders fell, her arms going slack at her side. "Then yes, you would have."

Her lip trembled a moment before she turned and walked away, stopping at the counter that ran along the side wall. "I've always loved you, Matthew."

He felt gut-punched at her softly spoken words. "I know you have."

She turned her head, tears swimming in her eyes. "You never loved me though, did you?"

He didn't answer. He'd hurt her enough. She didn't need to hear the truth from him. His actions were proof enough. Had he loved her, he would have married her years ago.

She picked up something from the counter and crossed to where he stood, grabbing his hand and laying it in his palm. "This just came in yesterday. It's the nicest brooch we've ever had. I think it would make a lovely Christmas gift for your new bride."

The corners of her mouth turned up into a smile but he could tell it was strained. He closed his hand over the brooch and leaned down, placing a kiss to her cheek. "You're a good woman, Cora. You'll make a fine wife to someone one day."

She nodded, those tears in her eyes falling and he reached up to brush them away but she stepped back and swiped at her cheeks with both hands, smiling when she looked back up at him. "It's late. I should be getting home."

Matt nodded and held up the brooch in his closed fist. "I'll be by later in the week to settle with you for this."

She waved a hand in the air, dismissing his words. "Consider it a wedding gift." Her smile widened as she met his gaze, the sadness still in her eyes telling him the smile was forced. "I hope she makes you happy, Matthew."

"And I wish the same happiness for you as well."

He left her inside the store alone when she refused an escort home, and crossed town to the mercantile, collecting the tea service and the tea tins and was headed back home by the time the sun started to lower over the mountain. The conversation with Cora hadn't been as hard as he'd thought it might be. Surprisingly, she'd been quite civil about it in the end.

The brooch she'd given him was a peace offering. He pulled it from his coat pocket. It was a nice piece. The cameo was in ivory and small pearls encircled the entire thing with a larger one hanging from the bottom. He was sure Julia would like it. Most women would. But giving it to her at Christmas ...

The very thought of celebrating made him uneasy. How could he laugh and be happy when his own negligence cost the lives of two people he'd loved? He hadn't acknowledged the holiday since that winter four years ago and he didn't want to do so now, but he knew Julia wouldn't accept that there would be no Christmas for them.

He gave the brooch one last look and pocketed it. He'd have to tell her what happened. Her bringing a tree into the house and collecting pine boughs were enough to tell him she wanted to celebrate. Him telling her no and tossing the tree out wasn't enough. She deserved an explanation. He just hated dredging it all up again.

By the time he made it home, it was near dark, which was why seeing Prudence heading to the barn surprised him. She stopped and watched him cross the bridge, then hurried to the barn and flung the doors open.

He rode inside and was on the ground undoing all the saddle cinches when she reached his side. Her arms were crossed over her chest, fire shining in her eyes. "Whatever it is Pru, save it. I've had enough drama today to last me clean into next year."

"Your wife is leaving."

His hands stilled on the worn leather straps, his heart skipping a beat at her words. When he looked over at her, her lips were near white she was clenching her mouth shut so tight.

"Why have you not consummated your marriage yet, Matthew? What are you waiting for?"

He'd never heard his sister talk about something so intimate as to what went on behind a man and woman's closed bedroom door and her mentioning it to him made his face burn hot. He opened his mouth to say—what, he had no idea—but she cut him off before he got the first sound out.

"Don't try to deny it. I know what's been going on around here. Or what's not been going on, I should say. Did you know your wife thinks you don't like her? That you're in love with Cora?"

In love with Cora? His confusion must have shown as she said, "Julia thinks the reason you've not come to her is because you're in love with Cora and that you can't bear the thought of touching her because of it."

"Why would she think that?"

"Because that hateful old bitty came all the way out here to tell her so!"

Now he was confused. "Cora was here?"

"Yes."

"When?"

"This morning."

He'd spent the morning with the sheriff, riding the pastures to show him where the wolves had attacked the younger cow and warning him about the possibilities of more of them roaming the valley. They'd ridden the fence line half the morning looking for tracks but never found more. "I just talked to Cora. She never mentioned being out here."

"I don't suppose she would. It wasn't you she wanted to see, it was Julia."

"Why?"

"To stir up trouble as always. Julia said Cora told her she wanted to talk to you and when she found out you weren't here, she said she'd wait until you got back. The hateful thing then told her you two were engaged and left before Julia could say a word about it, which tells me, her intentions were to hurt Julia, not talk to you."

He sighed and ran a hand over his face. Could this day get any more miserable?

"Where have you been sleeping?"

He finished unhooking the buckles holding the saddle on. "In the small room off from the kitchen."

"Why?"

"Not that it's any of your business, but I didn't think Julia wanted a complete stranger in her bed." He finished unhooking the straps and pulled the saddle off the horse's back, laying it across the railing.

He turned to face Pru, her scowl still in place, and he crossed his arms over his chest. "Tell me, Prudence, if you had traveled nearly the entire length of the country and married a man you'd never set eyes on before, would you have wanted him knocking on your door once the sun went down?"

She didn't answer but he hadn't really thought she would. "We were strangers, Pru. Hell, we still are for the most part but don't think for a moment that just because I haven't walked up those stairs to her room that I don't want to, because I do. I just didn't think I had a right to."

"Why? It's been four weeks."

"I wanted her to be comfortable and—"

"And what?"

He blew out a breath. "I wanted her to want me there."

She stared at him for long moments, then nodded her head. "Well, I think it would be safe to climb those stairs, now." She crossed to where he stood and laid a hand to his arm. "She's very confused and hurt and thinks you don't even like her. Bed your wife, Matthew, and tell her why you behaved like a lunatic today. She deserves to know."

He knew without asking what she was referring to. That same sad look he saw in her eyes every Christmas was there again and he knew she was feeling the loss as much as he was, if not more.

"I'll tell her." He leaned down and kissed her forehead and helped her saddle her horse, then watched her cross the bridge and head up the road. He stood there until he could no longer see her, then turned back to the house.

CHAPTER NINE

The kitchen door opened as Julia began setting out the food. She didn't spare Matthew a glance as he washed his hands, nor when he crossed the room to the table.

The meal she'd fixed was simple fare, and in her current mood, it had been a struggle to even prepare what she had. The day had been draining. The visit with Cora had been eye-opening and her conversation with Prudence exhausting. She'd nearly made her mind up to leave before her sister-in-law had shown up but now she wasn't so sure she should. Prudence had assured her that Matthew wanted her there. That he didn't love Cora as the woman had said he did.

Matthew sat down without a word and they ate in silence, neither one saying a word. He barely acknowledged her and every bite she took seemed to get harder to swallow. She pushed her food around on the plate more than she ate it. Between cooking and sitting down, she'd lost her appetite.

Her heart felt so heavy. No matter how hard she tried to convince herself Cora meant nothing to her husband, him never coming to her bed was telling. He hadn't come to her for a specific reason and whatever that reason was, she wasn't sure she wanted to know.

Matthew's reaction to the tree wasn't far from her thoughts either. She hadn't given much thought to Orin's questions about the tree but had noted he'd seemed a bit surprised she was putting one in the house. After seeing Matthew's reaction, she now knew why. Everyone seemed to know something she didn't and feeling so left out was upsetting. She felt out of place. As if she didn't really belong despite her best intentions.

Matthew finished eating and her plate had barely been touched. She stood to clear the dishes away but Matthew grabbed her hand before she could pick up his empty plate. "Sit down, Julia. We need to talk."

Dread caused her stomach to roll as she sat back down. Matthew pushed his plate away, then picked hers up and moved it out of reach. He folded his arms on top of the table and stared at the tablecloth for long moments before lifting his head to look at her.

He searched her face but she wasn't sure what he was looking for. "Pru said Cora came by today."

It took everything in her not to look away. "Earlier this morning when you and the sheriff rode out to the pasture."

"Cora is—"

"—You don't have to explain."

"I know but I'd like to anyway."

He told her what Prudence had earlier, and despite Cora's claims, Matthew didn't act as if he was thrilled at the prospect of marrying her. That, at least, lightened some of the heaviness in her chest. He'd seen her while in town, he'd said, their conversation more closely guarded but he assured her there were no hard feelings, that Cora wished them well.

When he mentioned the incident with the tree, he grew quiet, the look in his eyes distant. He stared at the table for long minutes before looking at her and saying, "I'm sorry about what happened earlier. You deserve an explanation for my reaction to seeing the tree. You did nothing wrong in bringing it in, I just reacted badly to it."

He looked away, a muscle in his jaw ticking before he met her gaze again. "Pru and I, we've not celebrated Christmas in four years. More often than not, I try to forget its Christmas time at all. This time of year is full of memories I'd rather not think about and seeing that tree—"

He ran his hand through his hair, his voice lowering in volume. "The bridge that crosses the creek is new. It took a long while to build but its sturdy now, so much so I can run my entire herd over it and not be afraid of it buckling under their weight. But, it wasn't always that way. Before that Christmas four years ago, it was weak and unsteady and I'd been meaning to fix it but never got around to it. There was always something else more pressing to do, so I kept putting off the repairs, intending to get to them when I had more time.

"My negligence cost Pru and me everything. A flash flood brought a small river of debris down the creek and when it hit the bridge, we heard it crack all the way on the other side of the barn. We all went running and reached the back of the house in time to see the support beams bow. The bridge swayed and—"

He shook his head, his eyes unfocused as if lost in memories he didn't want to remember.

"My father was on the bridge. He'd been coming back from town and his wagon was full of feed. When the bridge started moving, the horses got spooked and instead of running, they reared and danced in place. Jonas, Pru's husband, was closer and ran to help get them under control and off the bridge. I never made it. I was less than a dozen steps away when the entire thing went down, my pa, Jonas, the horses and wagon all swept away. It took us six days to find their bodies."

The images playing through Julia's head were probably lacking in most of the horrific detail that actually took place but tears still stung her eyes. Abe told her something had happened and that it wasn't his place to say what it was. Seeing that look on Matthew's face, she was almost sorry he'd even brought it up.

Had he been living with this pain and trying to ignore it all this time? His reaction to the tree said he had. "It's all right, Matthew. We don't have to celebrate. I—"

"—No," he interrupted, looking up. "It's not all right. I'll not force you to pretend as I've been doing and I'll never be able to tell you how sorry I am for the way I behaved earlier today. I'm not a violent man, Julia, I—" He paused and looked away for a brief moment. "I was scared. Hearing you scream and seeing those wolves, seeing the blood on the ground and thinking it was yours … It scared ten years off my life. Losing my pa and Jonas at Christmas, then losing you not two weeks to the day it happened? It would have been too much, and I overreacted. I never should have yelled at you." He reached out and took her hand. "I rarely ever raise my voice. I certainly didn't mean to today. I can only imagine what you think of me now but know this—I will never hurt you. Ever. I don't want you to fear me."

"I don't."

He nodded and smiled, giving her hand a small squeeze. "I'll help you put the tree back up tomorrow and take you to find more pine boughs." He stood and grabbed their dirty plates. "I'll clean this mess up, too. You go on up and get ready for bed."

Julia stood when he turned and carried the dishes to the counter, then came back to the table for the rest. She left him in the kitchen and climbed the stairs, feeling somewhat better than she had before their talk.

He didn't want Cora, despite what the woman had told her. But that didn't mean he wanted her, either. He told her why he'd reacted the way he had over the tree and she understood. Fear was a powerful emotion. She knew. She'd been living with some form of it since telling her father goodbye and getting on the train.

She spent long minutes undressing and washing in what remained of the cold water left in the pitcher on the dresser. She rubbed the sweet-smelling body lotion into her skin just like she did every night and put on her gown, then brushed out her hair and stared at her reflection in the mirror, again wondering why she even bothered.

Then there was a knock on her door.

"Can I come in?" Matthew wasn't sure she heard him, it was so quiet on the other side of the door, but long moments later, her soft reply of, "yes," told him she had. He turned the doorknob and stepped inside the room to find her by the dresser.

Her hair was down. It was the first time he'd ever seen it not pulled up into that braided knot she kept pinned to the nape of her neck. It fell down her back all the way past her waist, the firelight dancing off the curls as they brushed her hips.

She was half turned toward the door. The gown she wore was sheer enough he could make out the curve of her breasts through the material, their fullness drawing his attention to her nipples which were pebbled in the chilled room.

Her waist was thin, her legs impossibly long and he'd never seen anything so beautiful in his life. She was lovely and he'd lost weeks assuming she wanted time to adjust to being a new bride when all he'd had to do was ask her.

"Is everything all right?"

Her voice brought his eyes up. "Yes … and no." He took a step further into the room, stopping at the foot of the bed. "I've made a mess of things, Julia, and we've both suffered because of it." He inhaled deeply and glanced around the room, stopping when he spotted her trunks along the wall. He nodded toward them and said, "Prudence is the one who sent for you, not me. I only found out about you when your trunks arrived." He took another step toward her. "I showed up at the church that day to tell you there had been a mistake, that I couldn't marry you but —I wanted you the moment I saw you. You took my breath away."

She was quiet for a long while before finally saying, "Then why?" and turning to face him. "Why sleep elsewhere?"

"I wasn't sure you wanted me here." He scratched his eyebrow with his thumb. "Honestly … I was scared. Scared of being rejected by you. Scared you'd allow me to stay and I'd do something to frighten you or hurt you."

She took a few steps away from the dresser and the light from the fire gave him a peek at everything that gown was meant to show him. He looked his fill, his gaze lingering on her breasts before lowering to her small waist, to the flare of her hips and that small, dark triangle at the apex of her thighs.

"Me not coming to you had nothing to do with you, Julia. Don't ever think it did because I wanted you. I still want you. I've felt like a man possessed with the thought of you and I was just waiting for some sort of sign you wanted me in return." He looked down the line of her body again. "Because truth is, I'd very much like to share a bed with you, but only if it's what you want as well."

Her chest was rising quickly with every inhaled breath. He was making her nervous, could see it in the small tremble of her fingers. "It doesn't have to be now," he said, taking a step backward toward the door. "Whenever you're ready." He turned to leave but stopped when she said, "Don't go."

Matthew looked back over his shoulder. She'd taken another step closer to him, her chest still rising and falling rapidly.

"I'd like for you to stay." Her voice trembled and she brought a shaking hand up to her chest, her gaze darting to the bed and back as her cheeks darkened to a rosy pink.

She'd finally given him that sign he'd been waiting for and he closed the door, slowly crossing the room to where she stood.

Her eyes were a bit wide, her lips parted, and he raised his arm, laying his hand to her cheek.

Her skin was as soft as silk under his fingertips. He ran his thumb over her bottom lip and her eyelids closed. His pulse leaped as he brought his other hand up, lightly touching her other cheek, then the column of her neck and collarbone, stopping when he reached the small tie on her gown.

Some flowery scent clung to her skin and he breathed it in deeply as her eyes opened. He hesitated, that small silk ribbon holding her gown closed between his fingers and waited until she gave him a small nod of her head before pulling the string, the bow coming undone. He parted the material, exposing her breasts, his body reacting instantly and he froze, taking several deep breaths to try and calm down.

"Is something wrong?"

He shook his head. "No." He stared down at her, unsure if she wanted him to touch her or not and got his answer when she grabbed his hand and guided it inside the fabric of her gown. He cupped her breast, his thumb brushing over her nipple. "Everything is perfect," he said, before lowering his head to kiss her.

Her heart had been fluttering wildly as Mathew touched her but now, as he leaned down, his mouth inches from her own, she feared it would burst through her chest and the moment his lips touched her own, Julia forgot how to breathe.

She'd dreamed of being kissed by him, wondered what his hands would feel like against her skin and those dreams paled in comparison. There was a dreamy intimacy to the act and she felt drugged the moment his tongue touched her lips. Her womb clenched tight and a small moan crawled up her throat before she could stop it.

His thumb brushed her nipple again, the resulting tingles

shooting straight to her core igniting every nerve in her body. His breath was warm against her lips, tiny pulses of pleasure coursing through her veins as he pulled her tight against him. The evidence of his desire was felt against her leg and a moment of fear made her pull back.

He looked at her, his hand cupping the side of her neck before he leaned back down. His kiss was surprisingly gentle, his tongue dipping inside her mouth to taste her in slow, lingering strokes that made her heart race and caused heat to pool between her legs.

She wrapped her arms around his waist and she pressed her leg against his erection, earning a small moan from him in the process. She wasn't sure what she had expected to feel when Matthew finally came to her but this dizziness had never entered her mind. Her limbs felt shaky, her stomach doing little flips and each swipe of his tongue against her own sent more of those tingles racing down her spine. She felt weak, her mouth burning with fire and she wasn't close enough. She bunched the material of his shirt into her hands, leaned against him and kissed him back with a crazed sort of intensity that made her feel as if she was no longer in control of her emotions.

He broke the kiss a few moments later, panting out harsh breaths against her kiss-swollen lips and braced his forehead against her own. His hands moved to her shoulders, to the fabric of her gown. "Can I see you?"

She nodded and watched his face as he leaned back and pulled the gown down her arms, the material pooling on the floor at her feet. He took in every inch of her, his hands following the path of his eyes. "You're the most beautiful thing I've ever seen."

Julia felt a pleasant sort of heat wash over her from head to toe at the compliment, but embarrassment followed as he stood there staring at her. Matthew's gaze roamed the length of her body one last time before he gave her another small kiss then lifted her into his arms her carried her to their bed.

CHAPTER TEN

Matthew wasn't in bed when she woke. Julia frowned and sat up, holding the blankets against her chest as she looked around the room. That familiar pain that was usually there when she realized Matthew hadn't come to bed was back and she tried to tell herself it meant nothing. That him not being there when she woke didn't mean she'd disappointed him and he'd left.

But it sure felt that way.

She smoothed her hair down and rubbed the sleep from her eyes, her thoughts going back to the night before. Despite her disappointment in Matthew not being there, she couldn't help but be stupidly happy. It had been perfect and she'd never felt so loved and cherished. It's what she'd always wanted when she'd dreamed of married life. She glanced beside her. She just wished Matthew had been there when she woke up. It would have been nice to wake in his arms.

She slid to the edge of the bed, threw back the blankets and started to rise. The door swinging open pulled a startled squeal from her and she snatched the blankets back up to cover herself.

Matthew gave her a lazy smile when he stepped into the room, his gaze lowering to her barely-covered breasts as he crossed the room. When he stopped by her side of the bed, she realized he was holding a tray. He sat it on her lap, then leaned down and placed a kiss to her forehead. "Breakfast in bed for my lovely wife."

She blushed. It wasn't that she was naked with nothing covering her but the sheets on the bed, or remembering what they'd done the night before. It was nothing more than pure delight, that and she felt silly for thinking he'd abandoned her when she woke.

The tray held nothing more than bacon and eggs, toast with fresh butter and honey and ... "Is that tea?"

"It is."

Her head snapped up. "We have tea?"

"We do now. I picked some up yesterday when I was in town. I wasn't sure how you liked it, though."

"The honey will sweeten it perfectly, thank you." The tea was in one of the regular mugs they used for coffee every morning but she didn't mind. Who needed china teacups anyway. It was the tea that was important.

She tucked the sheets underneath her arms and made sure it was going to stay before pulling the honey spoon out of its container and dribbling it into her cup and giving it a stir.

"I have a few things to take care of outside so eat and dress, then come find me and we'll go gather those pine boughs you wanted yesterday."

Her heart fluttered at the suggestion, then skipped a beat when he leaned down and kissed her, taking his time tasting her lips. When he pulled back, he said, "And good morning."

She giggled, then blushed for being so silly. "Good morning."

He gave her another quick kiss and left and Julia grinned through her meal. The marriage may have gotten off to a rocky start but Matthew had made up for it in a single night. The breakfast in bed was a nice touch as well and as she ate, and sipped her tea, she stared out the window and daydreamed about what their future would look like.

Of all the mornings to be needed for one task after another, it had to be this one. Matthew finally made it back to the barn an hour after leaving the house and walking inside to find Julia with the colt was enough to erase his foul mood.

She smiled at him as he shut the barn door. Her hair was once again pulled up and his fingers itched to twist inside those locks again. Every single moment from the night before came to mind and he debated on heading back to the house instead of traipsing off into the woods for sticks.

She turned her attention back to the colt. He wasn't sure if the joy on her face was due to seeing the horse again or if maybe he was the reason. He hoped it was the latter. He hadn't seen her smile like that in all the weeks she'd been here so it gave him hope that maybe things were as they should be.

"He's already been fed this morning but when we get back, I'm sure he'd appreciate some attention."

"He seems as if he would." The colt butted her hand with his nose, wanting to be rubbed. "He seems starved for it."

"There's too much to do around here to give him the attention he craves." He crossed the barn and stopped beside her, reaching over the rail to scratch the colt behind the ear. "He seems to want us around more than the others do."

"With no mother, I'd imagine he did."

Matt watched her pet the horse, took in her features as she smiled and talked to the colt and wondered why he'd waited so long to walk up those stairs. He'd been foolish, he realized that now. He'd lost weeks of time by assuming she didn't want to be a proper wife to him. Weeks he'd never get back now but he'd make up for them if it took him a lifetime.

"You're staring at me."

Her soft voice drew him from his thoughts. He smiled and tucked a strand of her hair behind her ear. "I suppose I am." She flicked a quick glance at him before her cheeks turned red. He held back a grin. "Ready for our walk to get the pine boughs?"

"Yes."

They left the barn and Matt stopped in front of the house to grab Julia's basket and his rifle. She looked at it worriedly when he came back outside. "Just in case," he said. "I don't want to be surprised by those wolves if they decide to come back."

"Do you think they will?"

He didn't want to frighten her with talk of dangerous animals but he didn't want her to be ignorant and not realize they were here, either. He offered her his arm and started for the trees. "The sheriff was here to warn me about a pack of wolves that have been seen roaming the valley but I already knew about them. I've been missing some cattle and the herd had roamed further than they usually did. When we went to round them up, we found a fresh kill. They took down one of the younger cows so when the sheriff showed up, we rode out into the pasture to see if we found any tracks. We found plenty, but they veered off in so many different directions they were hard to track."

"And then they found me."

It wasn't a question and the slight tremble in her voice told him she was still shaken by the attack. "Luckily I was near the house when I heard you screaming."

If he hadn't been—he shifted the conversation, the what-ifs about the wolf attack too frightening to even contemplate. "Tell me about Charleston? What's it like there?"

The smile that lit her face was one he hadn't seen before. "It's beautiful." She glanced at him, her hold on his arm tightening. "We lived in town and our house faced the harbor so we had constant ocean breezes in summer. The veranda on the house spanned the entire front and both sides and I could have sat there all day." She laughed. "Well, I did spend most of my day there when it was warm. I never grew tired of staring at the ocean."

"Sounds nice. I've always wanted to see the ocean myself."

She looked up at him, a hopeful expression on her face. "I'd very much like to visit again someday."

Could he leave the ranch long enough to make a trip like that? That look on her face wanted to make him try. "I'll do my best to get you back there one day."

"Oh, thank you!" She bounced on her heels and leaned up, kissing his cheek, then blushed like a virgin. He laughed and wrapped an arm around her, pulling her close. "You don't have to be embarrassed for showing me affection."

She stared at the buttons on his coat, her face turning a darker pink until he tucked a finger under her chin to bring her head up. Every memory he had of the night before came back in an instant. The sounds she made as he loved her. The feel of her hands on his bare flesh, the taste of her kisses—the way she begged for more.

He lowered his head, taking her lips again in the kind of kiss he'd been wanting since leaving her naked and warm in their bed. She opened for him eagerly, her tongue slipping into his mouth as her arms came up to wrap around his neck. She made those small moans he'd heard the night before and his need for her was overwhelming.

He broke the kiss to give her a chance to breathe and stood there panting, their foreheads touching. "Would it be unseemly for me to say I wanted you again."

She grinned. "It's not even noon yet."

"Hmm … my desire for you doesn't care what time of day it is." He kissed her again, lingering until she moaned deep in her throat.

Julia pulled away panting. "Prudence said she'd come to take me into town today so I could visit with my friends."

"I can take you into town anytime you wish. All you would have had to do is ask."

"I didn't want to bother you with something so trivial. I know you have things to do around here."

"Nothing you want is trivial, Julia. It would be my pleasure."

"All right then. After we've picked the pine boughs."

He leaned down and gave her another soft kiss. "And after I've taken you to our bed." He gave her another kiss. "Before noon." And yet another kiss. "And had my way with you." Her face glowed so bright red he laughed. "You are a delight, wife."

"And you are a shameless flirt, husband."

CHAPTER ELEVEN

Matthew wasn't finished "having his way" with her, as he called it, for a solid week, not that she was complaining. She'd been loved to the point of exhaustion, had most of her meals while in bed with him, and even spent an entire evening being pampered with a hot bath for two in front of the fireplace in their bedroom.

He'd put all his things into the dresser again and hadn't left her bed since the night he'd knocked on her door and asked to come in. He'd delegated most of the chores to the ranch hands in order to spend time with her and she couldn't have been happier.

They'd learned a lot about each other over the past week and she hoped her friends couldn't tell what she'd been up to. The smile on her face seemed to be permanent and she feared the moment they saw her, they'd know she'd just spent the past six days, more or less, naked in bed with her husband.

Of course, her friends were newly married as well. For all she knew, their husbands were as enamored with them as Matthew seemed to be with her.

Julia hurried down the stairs and into the sitting room, peeking out the window to see if Matthew had brought the wagon around yet and was reaching for her cloak when someone said, "That's some fine decorating you've done in here."

She squealed, and jumped, hand flying to her heart as she spun on her heel to find Abe in the center of the room, arms crossed over his chest, head cocked to one side. "Abe! You scared the devil out of me."

He laughed like he always did and gave her a wink, then studied her in that way he sometimes did. "You look different."

"Oh?" She patted her hair, making sure it was all in place. "How so?"

"I don't know, just—different. Something's changed. You're near to glowing."

She grabbed her cloak and wrapped it around her shoulders. "Well, I've done nothing different since the last time I saw you."

"Things been going good with you and Matt then, I take it?"

She blushed. "Is it that obvious?"

He chuckled. "I'd say so. You look younger and a whole lot happier than you did the last time I saw you."

"Well, the last time you saw me I had just been nearly killed and yelled at." She bit her lip, pushing the memory away. It wasn't one she liked to recall. "So," she said, "What brings you by?"

"Nothing in particular. I just like checking in on you to make sure things are as they should be and to make sure Matt's treating you like he should. The Bailey's have a reputation to uphold, you know."

"Well, I don't think Matthew's done anything to shame any of his relatives. And we're fine, thank you for asking. Everything is —perfect now."

"Well, that's good to know. Seems as if my job here is done."

"What exactly is your job around here?"

"Oh, this and that. I was known as a jack-of-all-trades. There weren't many things I couldn't do and that included burning a pan of biscuits every now and again."

She laughed as he headed across the room toward the kitchen, stopping to look back at her. "You take good care of him now, you here?"

"I plan on it."

Her attention was drawn to the front door as it opened. Orin stood grinning in the threshold. "Your chariot awaits, my lady."

Julia hooked the clasp on her cloak. "You sound as if you've read a book or two."

"As many as I can get my hands on."

"Well, that's wonderful to hear. I know exactly what to get you for Christmas now." She turned to tell Abe goodbye but found him already gone. She shook her head, wondering how anyone could be so quiet when they came and went and was still puzzling over it when Orin escorted her outside, then helped her down the steps as they were iced over in a few spots. He took hold of her arm when they were on the ground, helping her across the yard to the waiting wagon. She laughed at his behavior. "I'm sure I can make it such a short distance without assistance, Orin."

"Maybe, but I'm not taking any chances."

"Chances on what?"

That grin on his face widened. "Well, as long as you and Matt have been holed up in that house, we all figure there'll be a new Bailey in the family by end of next summer."

It took her longer than it should have to suss out what he meant and when she did, her face must have shown every ounce of her embarrassment. Orin laughed as Matthew jumped down from the wagon and walked her way.

"What did he say?"

She wasn't about to repeat it and shook her head. "Nothing worth mentioning." He lifted her up into the wagon and spent the entire trip into town telling her about life on the ranch, how the field behind the apple orchard fills with wildflowers for as far as you can see, and of the swimming hole in the creek behind the house. He'd built a table and benches for Pru years ago and sat them under the trees along the banks. They hadn't used the area once since they lost Jonas and his pa but hoped come summer, to have a good many picnics there.

By the time they reached town, she was eager for the spring thaw so she could explore the ranch properly, and since Orin mentioned it, she wondered what the summer would bring.

She placed a hand on her stomach as they rode to the livery stable, a secret smile curving the corners of her mouth. Could she be carrying already? It was possible. Matthew had barely let her out of bed since he'd come to her so yes—she could very well be carrying his child. Was that what Abe had meant when he said she looked different? Hope bloomed in her chest at the possibility.

The town was decorated with pine boughs and ribbons and with the snow still on the ground, it looked exactly how she'd always pictured Christmas should look. The only thing missing was the carolers and the tinkling of a bell as someone from one charity or another stood with a collection cup on the corner.

Matthew left the horse and wagon in the care of Willie at the livery stable, then took her to the only restaurant in town, a small eatery which boasted a "fine dining experience," complete with lace tablecloths and an imported wine, for those who could afford to purchase it.

He introduced her to every person they met and she'd never felt so decadent in her life. Having his attention was an addicting feeling and as much as her heart fluttered every time she looked at him, she knew it wouldn't take very long at all to be completely in love with her husband if she wasn't already.

When they stepped back out onto the sidewalk, a light dusting of new snow covered the street and flurries were still falling. "Will it be all right to stay or should we head home?"

Matthew looked at the sky. "The clouds aren't thick enough for it to be much. I think we'll be fine."

"What will you do while I'm visiting my friends?"

"I'll find something to occupy my time." He lifted her hand and said, "If we weren't on the street and in plain sight of anyone looking, I'd kiss you properly," before placing a soft kiss to her palm. "Tonight, though—I'll kiss you in all my favorite places."

He left her there on the sidewalk, her thoughts going back to all the places he'd kissed her over the past week, a few of which heated her face to the point her entire body felt hot and caused her pulse to race. She debated running after him and having him take her home but dismissed the idea. He'd think she was a shameless wanton for even suggesting it.

She headed across town, looking into the shop windows as she passed, her heart filled with so much happiness she was glad she'd let the others talk her into coming with them out here. If she hadn't, she'd still be in Charleston, wishing for a better life while doing needlework by the fire every evening. She had that now—and she had Matthew. This was the life she'd always wanted. This feeling of belonging to a community where no one was trying to bring you down. Most of the women in the circles she knew back home would step on anyone to get what they wanted but the people in Angel Creek all wore happy smiles and she'd yet to meet a single person who didn't have a kind word for her.

Julia turned the corner, trying to remember which street Prudence had told her everyone lived on, and her distraction caused her to run into someone. They collided with enough force she nearly toppled over and when she was steady on her feet she saw who she'd bumped into. "Oh, my goodness! Forgive me, Cora. Are you all right?"

As she stared down at the other woman, she remembered the conversation with Matthew and him telling her he and Cora had talked and that everything was fine between them. That she'd wished them well in their marriage in the end, so the look on Cora's face was confusing to her now. A cold, taut expression covered her face, the angry glint in her eyes freezing her in place.

Cora lifted a hand, wiping at her lip. It was then Julia saw the small bright red dot of blood. "So not only have you taken my fiancé but you wish for my blood as well?"

"I apologize. I didn't realize—"

"Of course you didn't." Cora glared at her, her gaze dropping to her cloak. Her face reddened as she stared at it, one side of her mouth twisted in annoyance. "Perfect, beautiful Julia, one of the lovely southern belles of Angel Creek. I'm so sick of hearing about you all! Sick of it! You five are all anyone talks about anymore. Those lovely ladies all the way from the east coast with their proper manners and enchanting accents." She sneered at her, her lip curling in disgust. "It's as if you can do no wrong!"

Julia opened her mouth but Cora took a step toward her, lifted her hand and pointed a finger at her before she could say a word. "Stay away from me, Julia, and don't step foot inside my shop. You've taken the most important thing in my life. I'll not give you a single thing more. I don't care if you do pay for it."

The pain Cora felt was obvious. It was in every line of her face, in the way she stood, and heard in every harsh word she spoke. But what was the cause of it? And why would accidentally running into her make her so angry?

Or was it something else?

Had Matthew not told her the truth about his meeting with Cora? Had he told her things were well just so she wouldn't worry? Not that it mattered. Either way, Cora's reaction now wasn't what she'd expected and if she had to live in this town, they needed to get along. From what Prudence had told her, Cora had very few friends. She knew from experience how a lack of support would turn one bitter. She'd known many ladies like that so maybe Cora just needed a friend.

She straightened her cloak and said, "I was on my way to Sarah's house for a visit. I'm sure she has a pot of tea on and if not, it won't take much to persuade her to fix one. Would you like to join me?"

Cora stared at her long moments before hissing, "I'd rather dine with pigs," her voice laced with contempt. She came at her and Julia tried to step out of her way but gasped when Cora reached out with both hands and gave her a hard shove off the sidewalk.

In seconds, Julia was on her back, staring up at the white-washed sky as snowflakes fell onto her face, something wet and cold seeping into her cloak and dress. Voices around her grew in volume until she saw a man peering down at her.

"Mrs. Bailey, are you all right?"

She was still stunned enough that his words didn't register immediately but once they did, she smiled. She'd never been called Mrs. Bailey before. "Yes, I think so."

He helped her off the ground and held onto her arm until she was steady and the crowd was growing as she stood there. Seeing their shocked faces, she puzzled over the looks until she heard Cora—wailing as if some tragic event had just occurred.

They all seemed to notice her at once, everyone on the sidewalk turning to look at her, Cora turning with them, that accusing finger once again raised and pointed her way. "She did it!"

The gasps and disapproving head shakes were odd until she looked more closely at Cora. Four bright red claw marks raked down the side of her face and her lip was bleeding freely.

Cora let out another wail before shouting, "She said she'd kill me if I spoke to Matthew again, then attacked me."

And as Julia stood there with absurd accusations hanging over her head, the optimistic hopes for life in that town crumbled into dust.

Something was happening on the other end of town. The hammering of the blacksmith, nor the men gathered around the shop talking could distract from the commotion, or the raised voices he heard, and the occasional scream from someone screeching like a dying cat echoed through the streets.

He turned with several other men and headed toward the far end of town to where all the commotion was. When they rounded the corner and saw the crowd, one familiar, tall figure standing in the street caught his eye. "Julia?"

Matt pushed his way through the crowd until he reached her side, the look of relief on her face when she saw him enough to knock the air from his lungs. She leaned against him when he reached for her, burying her face against his chest.

Her cloak was wet, as was the back of her head. "What happened, Julia?"

She mumbled, "It was an accident."

"What was an accident?" He looked to the sidewalk, scanning the crowd. Whoever was crying was concealed behind a mass of people but they all seemed to shift as one. That's when he saw her. Cora, bellowing to the top of her lungs.

She saw him at the same moment and lifted her chin, her mouth set into a harsh, angry slash. "Do you see what she did to me, Matthew?" She pointed to her face, the red slashes down her cheek bright against her pale skin. "She attacked me for no reason at all."

The red marks down her face were fresh, blood pulled to the surface of her skin but he had a hard time believing Julia was responsible for it.

He looked down at her, met her gaze, and knew instantly she would have never done such a thing. He'd learned a great deal about his wife over the past week and her sweet, gentle nature was one of her most endearing qualities. Even if Cora had provoked her, Julia would never have struck her, let alone clawed Cora's face that way.

"Can we go home, now, please?"

Julia was once again staring at his chest, her fingers clenched in the fabric of his coat.

"Why are you wet?"

"I found Mrs. Bailey laying in the street when I came around the corner."

Matthew looked up at the voice and found Joseph Hall staring at him. The old man walked these sidewalks endlessly for no other reason than he had nothing better to do. If anyone would have seen what happened, it would have been him. "Did you see anything before finding her?"

He shook his head. "Nope. Heard someone yelling though." He flicked a glance to the sidewalk. "Sounded like Miss Cora to me."

"It was me!" Cora pushed her way to the edge of the sidewalk. "She told me to stay away from you, Matthew, and to never step foot on your land again, then just—attacked me. I screamed, of course, then shoved her away. That's how she ended up in the street." She crossed her arms over her chest. "Just what sort of woman have you married?"

Multiple people started talking at once and Matt knew he'd never get to the bottom of it with so many people around, not to mention, Julia was obviously distressed with so many onlookers hovering nearby.

He wrapped an arm around Julia's shoulders and turned, looking up at Cora. "Unless you'd like to discuss this in private, we're going home. I'll not let my wife become a spectacle for the entire town."

"What's there to discuss? Your wife attacked me!"

"Would you like to press charges?"

Cora's mouth opened, then closed, her gaze falling on Julia. Matthew waited but when she said nothing, he turned and started leading Julia away. Neither of them spoke as they crossed town to the livery stable, or while they waited for Willie to hitch the horse to the wagon. When they were headed back across the prairie he reached out to wrap his arm around her and pulled her close.

"You want to tell me what really happened?"

She looked up, surprise shining in her eyes. "You don't believe her?"

He laughed. "Not hardly. Cora has always had an over the top reaction to things. Today proved she still does."

She went limp beside him, her head falling to his shoulder and he realized then how tense she'd been. Had she actually thought he'd take Cora's side in all this? Without even knowing what really happened, he knew, regardless of what occurred, Julia wouldn't be at fault for it.

Julia told him her version of events and he had no reason to believe it didn't happen just as she said. Her question as to why Cora would behave the way she had when he'd told her she'd wished them well, was as puzzling to him as it was her.

Prudence stepped out of the house when they pulled into the yard. Matt helped Julia out of the wagon and told them he'd be in as soon as he'd unhitched the horse and got him back in his stall. Orin met him at the barn doors, both of them working quietly to see to the horse and he was about to leave when Silas's voice drew him to a stop. He looked around the barn and finally saw him in the loft.

"What's all this?"

When Silas leaned over the crate he'd stored up there, Matt yelled, "It's breakable so be careful."

"What is it?"

He hesitated, then said, "Gifts—for Julia. For Christmas."

Silas and Orin both stared at him as if they'd never seen him before. He ignored their curious gawking and left the barn, pushing the doors shut behind him.

He and Pru hadn't celebrated Christmas in so long, gift giving felt foreign now. But—Julia wanted the type of Christmas she was used to, and if he had to guess, he'd say gifts were a part of it.

That reason alone was why he hadn't given her the tea set he'd bought for her, or the remaining tea. He'd only taken the one tin inside the house, saving the others to give to her on Christmas morning when he gave her the tea tray with its fancy teapot and cups. The brooch Cora had given him was in there as well, but after today, he'd head into town first thing in the morning to return it. If Cora was going to behave the way she had on that sidewalk earlier, he wouldn't put it past her to accuse him of stealing it—or rather, accuse Julia of taking it.

He stepped up on the porch and could see Julia through the window. She was smiling despite her day. Her hair was matted in the back from the melted snow and street sludge she'd fallen into. He'd see that she had a proper bath as soon as Pru left.

The thought brought a smile to his face, wondering how soon he could make his sister head for home.

Prudence gave her a wide-eyed look as she removed her cloak. "What in the world happened to you?"

Julia started to hang the cloak by the door, then thought better of it. It would have to be washed. "Matthew took me into town to see my friends and I ran into Cora on the way."

"And?"

"And she wasn't happy to see me."

"Obviously." When she said nothing else, Prudence sighed. "You might as well tell me what happened because I'm not leaving until you do."

Julia told her every detail she could remember, knowing Prudence would have spent half an hour getting every detail out of her anyway. When she'd finished, Matthew opened the door and stepped inside.

Prudence crossed her arms over her chest and glared at him. "I hope you told her off."

"Who?"

"Don't play dumb with me, Matthew."

He hung his coat and said, "I hate to disappoint you, Pru, but I didn't say anything to her." He crossed to the fireplace as Prudence sputtered—trying to find the right words to yell at him more than likely—as Matthew grabbed a few logs of wood and laid them in the fire. "Well, actually, I told her we'd discuss it in private if she wished but she never moved, so we left."

Prudence scoffed. "Well, no one would be privy to the spectacle if you held the conversation in private. I swear, Cora thrives on drama." She turned to look at her. "This, Julia, is why Cora has no friends. She's just—"

"—Lonely." Matthew and Prudence both stared at her, speechless. "I think she's just lonely."

Prudence opened her mouth, closed it, then said, "I don't think that's the word I'd use to describe her."

"I know people just like her," Julia said. "They're hurting for one reason or another and lash out as a way to feel something." She met Matthew's gaze. "If it would be all right with you, I'd like to try to befriend her."

"You don't need my permission to be anyone's friend, Julia."

She gave him a grateful smile and saw a twinkling of light by the tree, her attention drawn to it. Seeing the tree reminded her of the party Cora had mentioned. "Were you planning on attending the Christmas party in town?"

He looked uneasy but said, "If it would make you happy."

"It would."

"Very well, then, we'll go."

Julia could tell the idea wasn't something Matthew wanted to think about but for her, he was willing. "I'm sure my friends will be there and it will be the perfect opportunity to introduce them to Cora properly."

Prudence made a choking sound. "You're serious about being friends with her?"

"Yes."

Prudence looked at Matthew. He only smiled.

Her sister-in-law shook her head. "Matt, who does she remind you of?"

"Gramps."

Matthew winked at her as Prudence laughed and said, "Gramps would have loved you, Julia." Her eyes took on a far-off look as if assaulted by memories. "The man never met a stranger and he didn't have a single enemy. Those who were most ornery around him, he sought out. Said everyone deserved a second chance and he gave them freely. He laughed often and loved scaring the snot out of me." She grinned. "I miss him every day."

"He sounds delightful."

Prudence turned and stared at the tree. "He loved Christmas time. Gran died when I was a baby so I don't remember her but Gramps said she always decorated the house and made sure we did every year after she was gone." She looked around the room. Julia did as well. The tree had been strung with homemade decorations and ribbons. The mantle adorned with pine boughs and dried berries. It wasn't as festive as the holiday decorations back home but for their first Christmas, it would do. "He would approve of what you've done in here."

"I'm sorry I never got a chance to meet him."

Prudence crossed to the small room behind the stairs. Julia had peeked in once, finding nothing but a small desk and stacks of ledgers. She could hear the shuffling of things, and a drawer opening and closing before Prudence came back, something in her hand.

"This is him."

Prudence handed her a small photograph within a tin frame. An older man with a shock of wild hair stood staring back at her. Julia's heart skipped a beat as she looked at his face. "What was his name?"

"Abraham, but everyone called him Abe."

117

Julia's heart started racing so fast, she felt dizzy and grabbed hold of the chair beside her to keep from falling down. She stared at the photograph of Abe, at the same mischievous grin she remembered, and barely heard a word Prudence was saying. She caught the word, "trickster," though and smiled. Yes, that was him, in a nutshell.

"He loved scaring people." Prudence moved to the tree and retied one of the bows on the branches, telling her of her grandfather's antics and Julia saw the small twinkling light again. As if by magic, the shadowy outline of a person appeared in the corner, the form slowly gaining substance until Abe stood there staring at her. He winked, and as quickly as he'd appeared, his image faded into nothing.

Well, that certainly explained how he came and went so quietly.

Matthew's arms closed around her from behind. "She's right, you know."

She turned her head to see him. "About what?"

"About Gramps. He would have loved you." He took her chin by two fingers and turned her head and placed a soft kiss to her lips, the arm he had draped around her waist tightening as he whispered, "Almost as much as I do."

CHAPTER TWELVE

Christmas Eve, 1914...

"That's it?"

Julia laughed. "Yes. What more do you want?"

The girls shifted in their seats, the oldest of them shaking her head before saying, "What happened with Cora?"

"And what about the party?" Emma squealed.

"Did you really see a ghost?"

The questions came at her so fast, she lost track of who asked what. "The party was amazing," she told them. That first Christmas party in town was one of the happiest she remembered. Matthew had even seemed to enjoy himself despite the fact she knew he'd only gone because she'd wanted to. Him going just to please her had endeared him to her and she knew without a shadow of a doubt that she loved him and told him so under a cluster of mistletoe someone had hung as a party decoration.

He'd kissed her right then and there, that public kiss earning them both a chastising from Prudence, who herself was chastised for interfering in the kiss by a man none of them had ever seen.

He'd been new to town, only arriving the day before, and if she had to guess, she'd say it was love at first sight for Prudence and Franklin. They'd been married less than two months later.

"Did you and Cora become friends?"

Julia was drawn from her musing by Rebecca's sweet voice. "Not exactly," she told her, "But, I spoke to her whenever I saw her and invited her to tea many times. She never lashed out at me again but she never accepted any of my invitations."

"Did she keep running after grandpa Bailey?"

Julia smiled. "No. She never spoke to him again as far as I know and eventually married a man who supplied items for Thompson's store and moved away the following year."

As if conjured by thought alone, Matthew walked into the room, a cup of punch in one hand, a small stack of molasses cookies in the other. He was still as handsome as he'd always been, even though his hair was mostly white now. He looked so much like Abe, and just like his grandfather, he was always right. He'd told her their life would be wonderful and it was. It had been filled with love and laughter, their home always full of happy noise, even when their children were grown and out on their own. Grandchildren had filled their days then and every year that passed, the Christmas season got easier for Matthew to endure until he was able to enjoy it again without guilt.

"She's doing it again."

"She always looks like that when she looks at grandpa Bailey."

The girlish giggles drew her attention and Julia tore her gaze from Matthew and looked back down at the small faces staring up at her. She turned to the others, her best friends in the entire world as they sat looking back at her. They shared a smile before she stood. "That's enough about me, children. Go pester aunt Ruby and have her tell you the story of her adventures in the army camp."

As the children all turned to Ruby, Julia crossed the room to where Matthew was standing, taking his cup to get a sip of punch to moisten her throat.

"Do you ever get tired of telling that story?"

"Never," she said, leaning up on her toes to kiss him. "I'll tell it every day if asked to. I never get tired of remembering our life together."

"Do you have any regrets?"

"Only one."

Matthew ran a finger over her cheek. "And what's that?"

She smiled and glanced back over her shoulder to make sure no one could hear her, then said, "Only that your stamina isn't what it used to be."

He laughed loud enough to draw the attention of half the people in the room but ignored them all, wrapping her in his arms and hugging her close. "Well, as soon as we get home, I'll see what I can do about that, Mrs. Bailey."

Julia grinned and gave him another soft kiss. "I can hardly wait, Mr. Bailey."

Dear Reader,

I hope you enjoyed Julia, the second bride featured in the Angel Creek Christmas Brides series. If so, please consider leaving a review.

Sweet romance isn't something I write very often. I like seeing those intimate moments between the hero and heroine and this story was no exception. I initially wrote about Matthew and Julia's first time but deleted the scene from the book. It wasn't very long, around 700 words in total and it's very mild compared to my usual sex scenes. I guess you could say it was a 'sweet' sex scene. I've placed it on my website, on a locked page, so if you would like to read it, you can find it, here: https://lilygraison.com/**bonusscene**/

The password to access the page is: *first kiss*

If this is your first time reading one of my books, I invite you to read my historical western romance, Willow Creek Series. These books are very spicy so if you prefer 'sweet' reads, these aren't for you, but … if you like naughty cowboys who always get their way, THE LAWMAN, book 1 in the series is FREE at all ebook retailers. Find the link to your favorite store here: http://lilygraison.com/TheLawman

Be sure to pick up Ruby, the next book in the Angel Creek Brides Series!

Five friends travel west to find love, what they don't expect is for the storm of the century to hit Angel Creek at same time. Snowbound with new husbands can pose quite an interesting turn of events.

After the Civil War, Charleston, SC is left devoid of eligible men. Ruby Henderson and four of her closest friends decide to travel west as mail order brides to find love. Upon arriving, she instantly regrets the rash decision. Especially upon meeting her husband to be who looks more like an outlaw, than a doctor.

Trevor Collins decides to put his distrust of women aside and marry. His new bride is more beautiful then he could have imagined, which makes him wonder about her true motivation for coming west. Will his wish to be a good family man win when the ugliness of his past rears its ugly head?

Even a giving heart has its limits.

Pick up your copy of Ruby here: https://amzn.to/2JnVlnW

Don't miss the other books in this series.

Book 1: Charity by Sylvia McDaniel: https://amzn.to/2DbWsXD

Book 4 - Sarah by Peggy McKenzie: https://amzn.to/2SsM9CP

Book 5 - Anna by Everly West https://amzn.to/2qisOr8

WANT MORE?

For information about upcoming books in the Willow Creek and Silver Falls Series, or any other books by Lily Graison, subscribe to her Newsletter or find her around the web at the following locations.

Website: http://lilygraison.com/
Newsletter: http://bit.ly/LilyNewsletter
Twitter: https://twitter.com/#!/LilyGraison
FaceBook: http://www.facebook.com/authorLilyGraison
Reader Group: http://bit.ly/LilyGraisonReaderGroup
Email: lily@lilygraison.com
Instagram: https://www.instagram.com/authorlilygraison/

Subscribe to email notifications of new releases here:
Newsletter: http://bit.ly/LilyNewsletter

Also by Lily Graison

HISTORICAL WESTERN ROMANCE
The Lawman (Willow Creek #1)
The Outlaw (Willow Creek #2)
The Gambler (Willow Creek #3)
The Rancher (Willow Creek #4)
His Brother's Wife (Willow Creek #5)
A Willow Creek Christmas (Willow Creek #6)
Wild Horses (Willow Creek #7)
Lullaby (A Willow Creek Short Story)
Nightingale (Willow Creek #8)
A Soft Kiss in Winter (Silver Falls #1)

SCIENCE FICTION ROMANCE
Dragon Fire (Prison Moon Series)
Warlord's Mate (coming soon)

CONTEMPORARY ROMANCE
Wicked: Leather and Lace (Wicked Series #2)
Wicked: Jade Butterfly (Wicked Series #3)
Wicked: Sweet Temptation (Wicked Series #4)
Wicked: The Complete Series (Books #1 - 4)

PARANORMAL ROMANCE
The Calling (Night Breeds Series #1)
The Gathering (Night Breeds Series #2)

STAND ALONE STORIES
Blame It On The Mistletoe (contemporary romance)
That First Christmas (contemporary romance)
Anna: Bride of Alabama (historical romance)
Julia: Angel Creek Christmas Brides (historical romance)

ABOUT THE AUTHOR

Lily Graison is a *USA TODAY* bestselling author of historical western romances. Her Willow Creek Series introduced readers to a small Montana town where the west is wild and the cowboys are wilder. Lily also dabbles in sci-fi, contemporary and para-normal romance when the mood strikes and all of her stories lean heavily to the spicy side with strong female leads and heroes who tend to always get what they want. She writes full time and lives in Hickory, NC with her husband and a house full of Yorkies.

Website: http://lilygraison.com/
Or Email Lily at: lily@lilygraison.com